The sound of skidding ti... street.

Dakota stiffened noticeably and barked. Daniel threw his arms around Aurora and propelled them both behind his SUV. Her evidence collection kit went flying.

"Dakota, come. Down!" Daniel shouted to the K-9.

Aurora's head was spinning. Her vision blurred. She fought to catch her breath.

Strong arms held her as Daniel shielded her with his own body and Dakota took a place on the ground next to them. Every muscle of the dog's massive body was tensed as if ready to launch an attack.

Time seemed to slow. The racing motor was so close. Shots cracked the frigid air. Daniel tightened his grip. Aurora had never been more frightened—or felt better protected.

* * *

DAKOTA K-9 UNIT

Valerie Hansen was thirty when she awoke to the presence of the Lord in her life and turned to Jesus. She now lives in a renovated farmhouse on the breathtakingly beautiful Ozark Plateau of Arkansas and is privileged to share her personal faith by telling the stories of her heart for Love Inspired. Life doesn't get much better than that!

Books by Valerie Hansen

Love Inspired Suspense

Undercover Escape

Dakota K-9 Unit

Final Showdown

Pacific Northwest K-9 Unit

Scent of Truth

Mountain Country K-9 Unit

Chasing Justice

Emergency Responders

Fatal Threat
Marked for Revenge
On the Run
Christmas Vendetta
Serial Threat

Visit the Author Profile page at LoveInspired.com for more titles.

FINAL SHOWDOWN

VALERIE HANSEN

LOVE INSPIRED SUSPENSE
INSPIRATIONAL ROMANCE

Special thanks and acknowledgment are given to Valerie Hansen for her contribution to the Dakota K-9 Unit miniseries.

LOVE INSPIRED® SUSPENSE
INSPIRATIONAL ROMANCE

Recycling programs
for this product may
not exist in your area.

ISBN-13: 978-1-335-95733-7

Final Showdown

Love Inspired
22 Adelaide St. West, 41st Floor
Toronto, Ontario M5H 4E3, Canada
www.LoveInspired.com

Printed in Lithuania

MIX
Paper | Supporting
responsible forestry
FSC® C021394

My times are in thy hand: deliver me from the hand of mine enemies, and from them that persecute me.
—*Psalm* 31:15

To family, born and adopted, and to those whose memories are the fuel that gently urges us to live the best lives possible in their honor.

ONE

Early snow had turned to slush on the sidewalks of Plains City, South Dakota, as autumn battled winter for dominance. Streetlights cast an eerie shadow on the multitude of footprints to and from the murder scene. Nothing about the modest house suggested the carnage inside but it was certainly there. A young woman had tragically been shot by her boyfriend. If it hadn't been for the statement from the witness next door, they might've never discovered who the murderer was.

Cold air hit Aurora Martin as she stepped out onto the porch and shed the protective booties that were part of her official investigative outfit as a crime scene tech. Her breath clouded. She stuffed the booties into the kit she carried, closed it, then zipped up her jacket and started toward the curb.

A deep male voice called from behind. "You can ride back to the station with Dakota and me if you like."

Turning, Aurora eyed the huge tan Great Dane at ATF Special Agent Daniel Slater's side, then noted his smile as he and his K-9 joined her.

"I don't bite," he added. "Ask anybody on my team. They'll vouch for me."

She couldn't help returning his grin. "It's not that. I have wheels. I borrowed my cousin Maddie's car while mine's in the shop getting a new starter." She gestured at the blue sedan parked behind his unmarked SUV. "See? Besides, I can't picture sitting there with my back to a K-9 big enough to put my whole head in her mouth."

As Aurora had intended, Daniel chuckled. "It's the drool that'll get you if you get too close."

"So I gathered." She glanced toward the modest home of the witness who had alerted 911 when she'd heard furious arguing and then gunshots coming from the house next door. "Are you sure Miss Effie will be all right?" The elderly woman had been Aurora's Sunday school teacher and was dear to her. Her description of the shooter she'd seen running from the house was a perfect match for Brandon Murray, AKA Jones, a notorious gun trafficker. The victim was his girlfriend, Lila Pierce.

Daniel nodded. "Effie will be fine. I'll see that she's looked after." He sighed, staring at the house. "Jones's prints are all over the murder scene because he lived there so they're useless as evidence."

"There's always ballistics," Aurora offered.

"With gun traffickers, that's not easy to track."

He was right. Trying to match ballistics would be challenging because traffickers had so many guns at their disposal—they could change them with the ease that people changed their clothes. It was a solid witness statement that would help the police get the killer. "True. Which brings me back to Miss Effie. I don't think she's safe staying here alone."

Daniel gestured toward a black-and-white Plains City police cruiser parked twenty yards up the street. "Don't worry. Your department has promised to keep a close eye on her until I can arrange witness protection with the US Marshal's office."

Aurora sighed. "I know. It's just that I care about her."

He arched a brow. "It's a long way from Sunday School class to crime scenes. What made you choose this line of work, anyway?"

"I'm not exactly sure. I've always loved puzzles and when it became apparent I didn't have the temperament to be a police officer, which was my first choice, I sort of drifted into forensics. It's fascinating. Sad sometimes, of course, but nevertheless absorbing." She gave him another smile. "And I still get to help put criminals behind bars." Maybe it was in her blood to fight for justice. After all, her cousin Maddie was a prosecutor for the district attorney's office.

"Once we catch them, you play a big part in getting convictions," Daniel said. "Too bad Jones is on the loose."

He looked frustrated by that. Everyone at the Plains City PD knew of ATF Supervisory Special Agent Daniel Slater, who'd been chosen to lead the Dakota Gun Trafficking Task Force which was made up of K-9 officers from various agencies across North and South Dakota. Their mission was to bring down a ruthless weapons trafficking ring that had been moving arms through the Dakotas and so far they'd made pretty good progress. Because the temporary DGTF headquarters was at the PCPD, Aurora had seen Daniel and his team around, though she'd never worked with him on a case. Until now. Unfortunately, the murder that had brought them together tonight had added yet another name to Brandon Jones's growing list of victims.

Aurora stepped off the curb when Daniel did, keeping him between her and the huge dog. She wasn't afraid of Dakota; she simply wanted to honor the fact that the K-9 was wearing her working vest and therefore not to be treated like a pet.

The sound of a revving engine and skidding tires caused all three of them to look up the street. Dakota was the first to stiffened noticeably. She began to growl.

Reacting, Daniel stopped and held up a hand in front of Aurora. She stared at the oncoming car. "What…?"

He shouted, "Dakota, come. Down," then whirled, threw his arms around Aurora and propelled them both behind his SUV. Her evidence collection kit went flying.

Aurora's head was spinning. Her vision blurred. She fought to catch her breath.

Strong arms held her as Daniel shielded her with his own body and Dakota took a place on the ground next to them. Every muscle of the dog's massive body was tensed as if ready to launch an attack. If the K-9 had not been so well trained, Aurora imagined she'd be on her feet snarling and barking.

Time seemed to slow. The racing motor was so close. Shots cracked the frigid air, punching a jagged line of holes in the opposite side of the parked car. Daniel tightened his grip. Aurora had never been more frightened—or felt better protected.

Engine sound peaked, then rapidly fell, indicating that the car had passed. Daniel released her, drew his gun and rested it on the hood of the SUV to steady his aim. The only thing that surprised her was that he didn't fire at the assailant's car.

The patrol unit that had been parked up the street sped past them in pursuit of the shooters while Daniel grabbed the mic from the radio in his car and began to report.

Suddenly on her own, Aurora trembled. Oblivious to the icy ground, she drew in her bent knees, leaned back against the side of the ATF agent's SUV and closed her eyes until she felt a weight against her shoulder.

The Great Dane had gently seated herself next to Aurora and gone into protection mode.

She was impressed. And surprisingly comforted. "Thanks, girl," she said quietly. "I owe you a steak later."

The massive head turned to look at her. Black accents on Dakota's muzzle and ears would have made her look fierce, especially since they were almost nose to nose, if Aurora hadn't sensed an emotional connection.

Instead of saying anything else, she tilted her head slightly and rested it against the dog's vest at the shoulder. Dakota could drool all she wanted as far as Aurora was concerned. She recognized a hero when she met one.

* * *

"The drive-by shooter may have been Brandon Jones," Daniel reported via radio, "or some part of the Jones/Murray gang." He looked back at the witness's house, expecting to see it riddled with bullet holes. It was not. Aurora's cousin's car, however, bore pockmarks in its door and front fender.

He shuddered when he realized how close the shots had come to the place where he and the crime scene tech had been standing mere seconds before.

A quick glance at the woman seated on the ground beside his vehicle calmed his fears. The assailants had been fast but he'd been faster, thanks in part to Dakota's immediate assessment of the situation. That was one way in which a canine's basic instinct topped that of a human. Most people stood and stared to consider approaching danger until it was too late to act, while a trained K-9 reacted immediately, even if the reason was not readily apparent. He'd learned long ago to listen to his dog and worry about figuring out the details later.

Holstering his gun, he offered a hand and spoke gently to Aurora as he pulled her up to stand beside him. "You okay? Not hurt?"

"As far as I know."

Concerned, he paused beside her. "Your cheeks are awfully red. Are you sure you're all right."

"I'm fine. Getting tackled knocked the air out of me, that's all."

"Sorry about that. Better a temporary discomfort than something more permanent, like a bullet, right? I'm afraid you're going to owe your cousin some auto-body repair work."

"As long as it's the car's body and not mine. Or yours."

"You're right about that." He pulled out his cell phone, punched in a text to his team and sent it before adding, "I think you should wait inside with the witness until backup arrives."

"What about you?"

"I'll be fine."

"Are you wearing Kevlar?"

"No, but Dakota is."

He almost chuckled at the way the pretty young woman rolled her hazel eyes at him. "I know she's intelligent," Aurora said, "but I doubt she's learned to use the radio or shoot back if something happens to you."

"I'll be safe enough here behind my car. It has extra reinforcement built in. And safety glass."

"No way," Aurora said. "You look smarter than that. Some calibers are capable of penetrating an engine block."

He hadn't expected her to argue and it took him aback. Daniel was not about to let her have the last word. "Magnums, maybe. Not what those guys were shooting. I could tell by the sound."

He saw her begin to frown as she added, "We can stand here and argue ballistics all day if you want. I'm right and you know it."

"And a little stubborn, maybe?"

Aurora shrugged. "Maybe."

Rising and falling siren wails signaled the approach of more backup units, giving Daniel a plausible reason to ignore any more unasked-for advice. It was less a matter of who was right than it was of maintaining control. He was the DGTF leader in charge of running the operation as well as looking into any tangential crimes that might affect the K-9 team's success at breaking up the gun trafficking ring. He didn't take orders from anybody except higher-ups at ATF, period, no matter what kind of attractive package they came in.

Two Plains City patrol cars approached and parked at a slant to block traffic, their sirens winding down, warning lights still flashing. His team was arriving. Detective Kenyon Graves bailed out of his K-9 equipped car and took temporary cover behind the open door. To Daniel's relief, US Marshal Lorelai Danvers was with him. Having her on scene was bound to expedite his request for witness protection for the elderly neighbor that Aurora was worried about. The second specialized car contained Jack Donadio who was finally off desk duty after recovering from a shooting injury.

"Stand down but stay alert," Daniel ordered his team. "And leave your dogs in the cars for now. This was a drive-by. There's nothing on the ground to track."

Kenyon straightened and holstered his gun. "Did you get a plate number?"

"No," Daniel said, looking toward Aurora. "You?"

"I was flying through the air, remember." The comment was delivered with the hint of a smile as she shook her head. "I did see a man looking out the passenger window and pointing a handgun at us just before I was knocked off my feet."

"That's something," Lorelai said. The tall blonde scanned the scene, her green eyes assessing. "Do you think you can identify him if you see him again?"

"Well, I don't think it was Brandon Jones," Aurora returned. "I've seen plenty of pictures of him. This guy was thinner, with narrowed eyes and a more pointed nose. Very scary-looking."

"Him or the gun?" Daniel asked. Judging by the tech's wide-eyed look, it could be either. He wished he'd at least gotten off a shot but protecting civilians came first.

"Not funny," Aurora said flatly.

"I wasn't trying to make a joke," he assured her.

"Color me skeptical," she countered. "I've been around enough cops to know gallows humor when I hear it."

"I'm saving that for later, after the crisis is past," Daniel replied. "Getting almost shot isn't exactly joking material."

"Then I apologize," Aurora said more softly. She took a step forward and leaned down to inspect the side of her cousin's car. "Maddie is going to kill me when she sees this."

"It's not like it was your fault." His brow knit. As he inspected the car riddled with bullet holes, he couldn't deny that it appeared this vehicle—or whoever was near it—was the intended target. Only that didn't make sense. Yes, the Jones gang had threatened Daniel and his team with revenge since the death of Brandon's brother, Hal, last month but there was no reason for this shooter to target Aurora specifically, was there?

"We'll be investigating the shooting but don't get complacent, okay? This looks intentional, as if you were the target. Can you think of any reason why or who might be taking potshots at you?"

"Of course not," Aurora countered. "They had to be after you. Your SUV is unmarked but there's no mistaking that K-9 of yours. She stands out no matter where you go or what you do."

Sighing, Daniel nodded. "That's true." He briefly introduced Aurora to his colleagues, then turned to speak to them. "Kenyon, you and Jack can return to headquarters as soon as this car is impounded for evidence. I need Lorelai to arrange witness protection for the woman in that house over there." He pointed to Miss Effie's place. "I'm going to take Aurora with me for the time being."

He paused long enough for the others to step away on their various missions before he looked back at Aurora. "Are you going to be okay or do you want to go to the ER for a checkup?"

"This isn't my first rodeo," she said flatly.

"No, but I suspect it may be the first time you've been caught in the line of fire. Am I right?"

Expecting a verbal answer, he was surprised when her chin jutted out and her eyes narrowed at him.

"What? Don't look at me as if I just called you a bad name. You're young. How much experience can you have had?"

"I'm twenty-seven."

"Really?" He'd have guessed early twenties at most. He hesitated long enough to sigh. "I guess everybody looks young at my age." Feeling old was new to him and he blamed the unexpected changes to his personal life for the change in perspective. Now that it looked as if he was going to be raising his half sister's little girl, he was suddenly seeing himself as belonging to an older generation, as if being a parent had aged him.

To his chagrin, Aurora chuckled. "I happen to know you're thirty-four. That's hardly old."

A slight smile twitched at the corners of his mouth and he let it blossom. "Maybe it's becoming an instant father the way I did that's made me feel so ancient."

"Life can be strange." Aurora's low voice cut through his thoughts. "Mine certainly has been." Judging by the way her smile faded and she averted her gaze, Daniel got the idea that he wasn't the only one dealing with personal problems.

He shrugged. "I guess the whole police station knows my story. It's hardly a secret what's been happening with my extended family." Having the thought felt bad but voicing it was worse.

"Believe me, I understand about family troubles. Been there, doing that," Aurora said, starting to walk away. There was so much pathos in her voice that Daniel decided then and there to find out exactly why. Granted, it was none of his business, yet there was something about this woman that made him want to help her and that began with trying to understand what made her tick.

He opened the rear of his SUV and gave Dakota the command to jump in. She sat patiently while he examined her paws for clumps of ice and dried them before joining Aurora, who had picked up her kit and made herself comfortable in the front passenger seat.

Daniel slid behind the wheel and turned the key. Aurora

was holding her hands in front of the vents and rubbing them together, clearly waiting for warmth to come through.

"Sorry," he said. "I would have started the car earlier if I'd realized you were cold."

He heard her sigh despite the purr of the engine. "I didn't realize how chilled I was until just now." She began to smile slightly. "I must have been a bit preoccupied."

Daniel grinned back at her. "Yeah. I'd say so. We'll want to get you set up with a forensic artist unless you think you can ID the shooter from mug shots."

"I'm less concerned about whether I can actually identify him than I am that he figures out who I am and *thinks* I can. Whether those bullets were meant for you or not, I may be a target now."

"Unfortunately, I agree." Checking his side mirror, he pulled away from the curb. "Where do you live?"

"I have an apartment on the west side."

"I wouldn't advise you to go anywhere near there." He paused, thinking. "We need to warn your cousin too, just in case you were mistaken for her."

"Whoa! Where did that idea come from?"

"I'm just considering all the possibilities. We can't count on the drive-by shooter just having bad aim. He may actually have been aiming at your cousin's car, intending to send her a warning."

"Why? Because she's a prosecutor for the DA?"

"She's what?"

"A prosecutor. I thought you knew."

"I do now. That's even more reason to think that her car may have been targeted. She has undoubtedly made enemies in her profession."

"Do you actually believe someone is trying to hurt her?" Aurora asked.

Daniel shook his head. "Anything is possible. Either way,

I don't think it's a good idea for you to stay with her—or any of your friends tonight."

"Not a problem," Aurora answered. "I can bunk at the station in the women's locker room. I've done it before when I was too tired to drive home."

What about a safe house?"

"No way. Those are for endangered citizens and witnesses. I'm not going to take up space someone else might need."

Falling silent, he stopped himself from offering her a room at his house. Yes, it was big enough, and, yes, it was well defended and secure. Nevertheless, there was a line he didn't want to cross; an undefined distancing he felt his job required.

He cast a quick glance at the young woman riding beside him. There was a vulnerability to her that touched him despite his determination to remain aloof. She had just put others first while he was in a position to help her and was holding back. That didn't speak very well for his character, job description or no job description. He should at least offer... She'd probably refuse anyway.

"Listen, my place is fenced and gated with alarms and cameras," he said. "There's plenty of room for you in a separate wing."

"A *wing*?" Her brows arched as she looked back at him.

"It's the home I lived in growing up. For all his faults, Dad managed his finances well." He swallowed the lump in his throat that formed upon mentioning his father.

"Then, yes," Aurora said.

Daniel stifled his surprise. "Yes?"

"Yes," she repeated. "It might be fun to see how the rich folks live."

"I'm far from rich," he said. "It's just a house. Okay?"

When she said, "Okay," and gave him a slight smile, he was sure he detected underlying worry that she was trying to hide. Despite her smile, he could tell the shooting had shaken her up much more than she'd admitted, which was probably why she'd agreed to stay at his house in the first place. Still, his place was the safest sanctuary he could think of and it was his duty to share it with someone in need. Never mind that Aurora Martin was personally more appealing than he was ready to admit to anyone, particularly himself.

Members of his team might be falling in love right and left but that didn't mean he'd ever consider marriage. As he saw it, his primary job was law enforcement and although his personal commitments now included raising his twenty-two-month-old niece, Joy, he saw no reason to complicate that relationship with a woman. His grandmother, Catherine, was already used to stepping in when he was away on assignment and that arrangement suited him just fine. Lots of kids were successfully raised by single parents and their extended families.

Thinking back to his own youth, Daniel clenched his teeth. Everyone would have been happier, in his opinion, if his father had *not* been in the picture, particularly given that man's philandering nature and unloving behavior when he did come home.

Picturing little Joy made him start to smile until he added his ailing half sister, Serena, to the remembrance. He could never make up for the way their father had deserted her but he'd promised to raise his niece with love and that was exactly what he intended to do. A natural extension of that vow was his determination to guard his own life so he could keep dedicating it to the innocent little girl. She deserved that, and more.

Which brought his thoughts full circle, back to the need to safeguard himself as well as those around him. As long as there was a definite threat from the gun trafficking gang, no one was safe. Not even a K-9 officer wearing a Kevlar vest. Not even a man who had vowed to become a better father than his own had been and raise little Joy with the love that had been denied him.

Daniel clenched his jaw. He'd always known the inherent dangers of a career in law enforcement and had accepted them as part of the package. Now, however, his mindset was changing to include self-preservation and given the chances of an encounter with the ruthless criminals he was pursuing, that ambivalence could prove more dangerous than an assassin's bullet.

TWO

Coming to a stop in front of heavy ornamental wrought iron gates, Daniel pushed a button and the gates slowly swung back.

Aurora didn't try to hide how impressed she was. "Wow."

"That's one way to put it. I told you the place was fortified."

"All it needs is a moat and a drawbridge and you'd have a castle," she drawled, leaning forward to peer at the imposing structure they were approaching. The front wall of the first floor was faced with rock while the rear had to be covered with soil because the house looked as if it had been tucked into the side of a hill. Columns supporting a wide porch marched in a line all the way across between that level and the second floor, which featured a peaked center and a bank of large windows.

"Those big windows up there don't look very private," Aurora said.

"It's deceiving. The upper floor makes the place look vulnerable. The ground floor windows are more like slits. See?" He pointed. "We can close them off and lock down that level like a safe room."

"The whole floor?"

Daniel nodded. "Yup. Who needs a moat, right?"

"I suppose." Thoughtful, she decided to ask a question. "I can understand why an ATF agent like you might want a secure home but you said your late father built this. Was he in law enforcement too?" Judging by the way Daniel huffed and the wry face he made, she'd guessed wrong.

"Dad was an investment counselor who later went into politics. I didn't know much about how he conducted business, but given the way he lied and cheated the rest of the time, I have to assume he was always expecting retribution of some kind."

"Sorry I asked," Aurora said with tenderness. "I didn't mean to remind you of past problems."

He huffed. "Since I'm probably going to be raising my niece here, I'll be facing the reminders of my dad's sins for the rest of my life. I've already come to terms with the past. It's certainly not the fault of Joy or her mother, Serena, who's gravely ill. It's too late to do much for her but I plan to do everything in my power to redeem Joy's future and provide the family her mom never had."

Aurora shrugged and offered a look of understanding. "I'm really not qualified to judge anyone's family. My own dad has been driving me crazy ever since my mom passed."

He sobered. "I'm sorry. I had no idea you'd recently lost your mother."

"Six months sometimes seems like ages ago. Other times, it's like yesterday." A sorrowful, tearful, painful yesterday.

"It's perfectly natural for your father to have a hard time adjusting," Daniel said.

Because he had stopped the SUV and was opening the driver's door, Aurora was able to turn away and keep him from reading the pain in her expression. Her dad had not only gotten over his loss, he'd started dating practically every woman in his life under seventy. As far as she was concerned, he was shoveling dirt on her mama's grave every time he wined and dined another woman. Not only were his actions embarrassing, it cut Aurora's heart to see him so keen on finding a replacement. As if Mama could ever be replaced.

Pausing beside the SUV while Daniel removed Dakota's

working vest and gave her the command to jump down, she saw the front door of the house fly open. A spry-looking older woman hurried toward them with a toddler in her arms. A plaid blanket wrapped around the child flapped in the breeze.

Calling, "Dan!" the woman enfolded him in an embrace that included the little girl and he reciprocated. Aurora felt like an intruder. The obvious love between them brought unshed tears that she quickly blinked away.

"I was so worried after I heard about the shooting," the older woman said.

Aurora could tell the agent was both flattered and a little embarrassed. "I told you to stop listening to police calls on that scanner all the time, Nana. I bought it so you could keep from worrying, not so you'd take on all the problems in the county." He stepped to one side. "I'd like you to meet Aurora Martin, one of the Plain City PD's crime scene techs. Aurora, this is my grandmother, Catherine, and Joy, the niece I've told you about."

Smiling and nodding, Aurora exchanged pleasantries while Joy waved pudgy arms toward Dakota as if she expected affection.

"Doh-dah," she babbled, "Doh-dah!"

"She's already calling you daddy?"

Laughing, Daniel took the child from his grandmother and cuddled her. "Nope. That's her interpretation of Dakota. She wants me to put her down so she can pretend to ride the dog." He focused on Joy. "It's too cold out here for you, honey. Come on, everybody, let's go inside and I'll explain what's going on."

Feeling a touch left out, Aurora fell into step behind the group. She had rarely sensed this much unconditional love, especially not in her own upbringing. Little Joy had faced difficulties already and was going to lose her mother to cancer any day now, yet these extraordinary adults were there for her, regardless.

The urge to phone her father arose. She refused to heed it. Until he began to act like the bereaved widower he was, she just couldn't bear to speak with him. Not when he sounded so happy about being alone and free to flit from woman to woman like a hungry bee visiting a flower garden.

Shivering, she wrapped her arms around herself. The temperature wasn't the only cold thing she was battling and she knew it. God had not answered her prayer to heal her mother and on that terrible day she'd felt as if she'd lost her father too. He was certainly different than the daddy who had raised her.

Closing her eyes for an instant she pictured the man, old, bereft, sharing her grief as she'd expected. But now? Now he looked and acted younger and much happier, as if he was celebrating being free from a marriage Aurora had always thought was good for both her parents. How could she have been so wrong?

Daniel was waiting by the sliding door on the lower level when she joined him. "Welcome to my humble home."

Two steps took her inside. Determined to keep from sounding like a kid at an amazing amusement park, she simply said, "Nice."

He laughed. "That's one way to put it." He gestured toward an interior staircase. "They've gone upstairs. It's more comfortable up there and Joy can play with Dakota while we talk."

"I need to take my boots off," Aurora said. "They're wet from the slush and they'll ruin your carpet."

"Whatever makes you comfortable," Daniel said pleasantly. "I can hang your coat up for you."

As he circled to help her, Aurora was suddenly aware of his presence in a way that left her a little unsettled. It wasn't merely because of being in his home; it was the man himself. His personal effect on her. The atmosphere and trappings of the lavish home might affect some people but she considered herself above that kind of influence. So, was it an aftereffect of the shooting? Was she recalling the feel of his strong arms bearing her to safety?

Daniel had taken her coat. She found a chair near the stone-paved entrance and sat down, preparing to remove her wet boots. Instead, he returned and knelt at her feet, gently easing the heel of one boot loose, removing it, then grasping the other.

"I can do that," Aurora began.

"You've had a rough day. Let me help," was all he said, yet it touched her to the core. It had been a long, long time since anyone had tended to her. The act was a simple thing, mundane really, so why did it bring tears to her eyes? Perhaps it was the contrasts she was glimpsing in the usually taciturn agent. Seeing his tenderness with the toddler was one thing. Having a taste of that same kindness toward herself was decidedly another. Too bad their situation was so fraught with danger and uneasiness. Under other circumstances, she could have relaxed and actually enjoyed the pleasant company.

Aurora shivered, recalling the shooting and the fright it had brought. Even amid the familial atmosphere, it was impossible to forget how close she had come to injury. Or worse.

The kitchen upstairs was brightly lit and his grandmother was busying herself preparing a light meal as coffee brewed. Daniel offered his guest a seat on one of the sofas. It didn't surprise him when she followed him into the kitchen instead and offered to help.

"I've got this," Catherine replied with a smile. "Have a seat. Do you take cream and sugar in your coffee?"

"Yes, please. Both," Aurora said.

Daniel carried two steaming mugs to the table, held a chair for Aurora, then joined her. He passed sugar and cream before using it himself. "Sorry, no artificial sweeteners. Nana's a stickler for healthy food."

"Works for me," Aurora said, pausing to take a cautious sip. "Good coffee."

"Low acid, no pesticides," Catherine announced as she approached with a tray of meats, cheeses and assorted crackers. "If you're like Dan, here, you miss half your meals. Let me know if you want anything else."

He scooted his chair closer. "I need to fill Aurora in on a few things."

Catherine glanced toward the toddler happily placing a line of blocks along the rib cage of the reclining Great Dane, giggling every time Dakota twitched and some slid off.

"It's somebody's bedtime so if you two will excuse me, I'll give our little one a bath and put her to bed," the older woman said.

Relieved, he started to relax. Wrapping both hands around the warm mug, he stared into the steam for a few seconds to gather his thoughts before asking, "How much do you know about the situation with my niece?"

"Only that she's the child of your half sister who is very ill and you're looking after her."

"Yes. Serena's terminal, I'm afraid."

"I'm so sorry."

The light touch of Aurora's hand on his gave unexpected comfort and he managed a slight smile. "It is what it is. She had a hard life even before she got sick. I'm thankful I can be there for her but I do wish we'd known each other as children. It might have helped now."

"Or made it worse," Aurora offered softly.

"How so?"

"I don't know. Maybe the lack of memories will end up being for the best. When I think of my late mother and all the lovely times we had, it hurts my heart.

"On the other hand," he said, "Serena and I had no chance to make good memories together and that can be even sadder."

"You're right. I'm sorry." She withdrew her touch and leaned back. "Go on with your story."

"I began looking for Joy's mother as soon as she left her outside the station with a note that said she was my kin. Joy had a birth certificate with her that gave Serena's name as her mother but nothing else. She'd dropped off the grid by then."

"You're sure you're related?"

"Yes. DNA proved it. When we finally did locate Serena, she was out of state and failing fast so I had her brought back to South Dakota where I could oversee her care in a hospice closer to home and family."

"Why did she leave Joy at the station ATF shares with the police instead of bringing her straight to you? I can't imagine leaving a child like that for any reason." Seeking something to do with her hands, she picked up a piece of cheese and nibbled it.

"Neither could I until she explained. She watched from across the street until somebody took Joy inside. Serena was alone and very sick at that time. She knew she wasn't going to be able to properly care for Joy much longer, and when she was accepted into an experimental drug program in Texas, she left her behind and went there, hoping for a miracle cure."

"Which didn't come."

Daniel sighed deeply. "Right. The drug trial ended without any positive results for Serena so she was ready to return to Plains City and see Joy again." The frown on Aurora's brow caused him to add, "I did clear it with Joy's pediatrician before I took her to visit her mother in the hospital. I was afraid the sight of Serena so sick might cause her emotional harm."

"He encouraged you to do it?"

"With proper preparation, yes. He explained that young children aren't hindered by adult logic. We spoke with Serena first, of course, and explained that we were planning to tell Joy about Heaven and why. She was more than eager to go along with it."

Aurora's hazel eyes glistened. "It's not a fairy tale. I truly believe there's a place in Heaven waiting for those who believe in Jesus and commit to Him."

"That didn't come out the way I intended," Daniel said quickly. "I wasn't making up a happy ending for Serena's story. I truly believe her pain will be gone in heaven and she won't cry for the earthly life and family she's lost, but you can't go into a lot of detail with kids who are barely making whole sentences. Later, when Joy is older, Nana and I can explain more fully. I'm just thankful Serena brought Joy to me, to us, and gave us a chance to help when she needed it most."

Thankfully, Aurora's features seemed to relax before she said, "Okay. I do see your point. So, how did it go?"

"Pretty well, actually. Serena shed some happy tears. We waited until she was moved to hospice so there wouldn't be a lot of noisy machinery. The atmosphere now is actually quite peaceful, considering."

"Peaceful?

"Yes," Daniel said with a sigh. "Nana and I alternate whenever possible and take Joy in only when the nurses advise us ahead of time that Serena is ready."

"I can't see how you could handle it any better," Aurora said. "Again, I'm sorry."

"Faith helps. I'm sure it was a comfort to you when your mother passed."

The attractive face that had begun to soften tightened in another scowl. "Yes, and no. I miss her terribly. It's too bad not everybody in my family does."

"You can't be sure of that."

"Oh?" Her eyebrow arched. "My dad has made it pretty clear to everybody in town. He's acting like a teenager who is suddenly off curfew, running around and chasing women right and left. Any female under seventy is fair game."

Daniel wasn't about to share all the details of his disillusionment with his own father such as his disowning Serena in spite of his paternity, then refusing to have anything to do with her even when she was grown and needed help but he did huff with derision. "At least your dad is single. Mine acted like that when he was very married."

Although he hadn't spoken with the intent of distracting his guest, his statement did just that. Lips slightly parted, she stared at him. Moments of silence passed until she asked, "You mean with Serena's mother?"

A nod was all that was necessary to bring their conversation to a permanent close. Reaching for the tray of food, he politely passed it to Aurora before taking some for himself. He'd already revealed a lot more about his dysfunctional family than he'd intended and was not about to continue.

Rumor had been running rampant ever since little Joy had been plopped down into his life and he was determined to get past it, for her sake. The most he could hope for was that he'd never follow in his father's footsteps and to guarantee that he fully intended to spend the rest of his life dedicated to raising his niece in a stable home among adults she could trust and rely on no matter what.

He'd seen lots of instances where single parents did wonderful jobs. Conversely, he'd seen supposedly happy homes dissolve like the last snows of winter beneath the bright sun of the Black Hills.

Joy was who mattered now. She had her whole life ahead of her, and whether he understood it or not, he'd been placed in her short life to guide and love her. The loving part was easy. It was how to best provide guidance that had him concerned.

First, I have to survive this job. And protect others who need me too.

"Daniel?" Aurora reached out and almost touched his hand. "What?"

She pointed to his pocket. "I think your phone is buzzing."

Surprised to have not noticed immediately, he turned away to answer. "Slater."

It was West Cole, a detective with the Plains City PD and a member of the task force. "Thought you should know," West began, "we're responding to the report of a suspicious vehicle that keeps cruising past your place. You might want to stay away from the windows until we're sure what's up."

"Yeah. Thanks." Daniel was about to explain to Aurora when a loud beeping sounded inside the house. He tensed, gripping the phone. "Alerts going off now," he told Cole. "Bump up response to code three!"

THREE

Aurora picked up on Daniel's changing mood instantly. He looked first at her, then at the stairway they had climbed to reach the open level. "Nana knows what to do in an emergency. You stick with me. My home office is down stairs."

Daniel led the way to a windowless room at the back. Not only did it contain a desk and a large enough table for team meetings, there was a bank of monitors on one wall that showed shadowy images of the outside of the house and grounds.

She didn't try to hide her amazement. "Wow."

"Home sweet home," he said, focusing on the live-action monitors. "I told you this place was well equipped."

"You can say that again." Something on one of the screens caught her eye and she pointed. "Look."

He barely glanced at her as he said, "I see—we've got company."

Circling to the desk, he stopped at a keyboard below the wall display and punched in a number. One screen zoomed in revealing a hooded figure just as it ducked behind one of the trees at the perimeter.

"That doesn't look like one of the local PD officers. Besides, they can't be here yet. This guy is inside."

"How would anybody know I'm here?" There was more

anxiety in her tone than she liked so she breathed deeply in an effort to control herself better.

"They may not be here because of you," he said. "My team has been targeted too, since the death of Brandon Jones's brother, Hal."

"The same Brandon we suspect of that murder we just came from?"

"One in the same. We think Brandon's brother, Hal, was the brains of a gun trafficking operation, but since his death, with Brandon going off the rails the way he has, it's starting to look like this case may be coming to a close—in a good way."

"But what about—?" was all she got out before Daniel raised a hand, palm out, to quiet her. He made a quick call while Aurora listened.

"Yes. That's right. To the west, just inside the fence." He paused. "All right. We'll approach from this side. Just tell your officers I'll be on scene with my K-9 so they don't shoot us."

Aurora reached to grab his arm as he strode past, thought better of it and stood back. "You aren't going out there?"

"Of course I am."

"But..."

"You'll be safe inside, and I'll be careful. I'm going to leave you locked in down here. As soon as I'm sure Joy and my grandmother are safe upstairs too, I'll see about the problem in the yard."

"What if—?" Aurora was getting tired of starting a sentence and having him signal her to stop talking.

"Watch the action on the monitors if it will make you feel more secure. Just do as I say and stay in this room."

An argumentative element of her personality urged her to snap off a mocking salute as Daniel left but she restrained the impulse. There were worse places to be left alone than this secured room. For instance, she could be upstairs where there was open access.

That realization caused her to pause in her selfish thoughts and turn her attention to the well-being of the others. "Father, be with them. Protect them. Please," she began, adding, "and forgive me for complaining about Your plans for me."

Her focus rose to the screens as she waited to see something, anything, that would put her mind at ease.

Long minutes passed before a door slammed upstairs. Floodlights illuminated the entire property. There he was. Daniel Slater. He was dressed in black but in the center of his back were the bright white letters *ATF*. They would keep him from being misidentified as the intruder but they would also point him out as a federal agent to anyone bent on causing harm. Trotting beside him in her K-9 vest, Dakota kept pace.

Aurora's head swiveled back and forth from one screen to another, searching for danger as if she could somehow warn her brave defender. She didn't even have his cell number to call if she did spot the adversary. Well, that could be remedied, and would be as soon as he returned.

"He'll be back. He'll be fine. I know he will be," she insisted softly to herself. "So will his K-9."

The words echoed in the empty room like a shout straight from her heart. This was a good man. He was needed by his fatherless, soon-to-be orphaned niece and by the task force.

And by me, she added, a bit surprised to identify so closely with the agent and his mission in life.

No, that's normal for me. I care about people. That's why I chose my job.

Starting to smile at the self-expressed argument, she caught a flash of movement out of the corner of her eye. There. By the wrought iron gate. It was Daniel, opening a pass-through for armed men on foot. Backup had joined him. Hooray!

She breathed a sigh of relief. Her shoulders began to relax. And then she checked a different screen and saw someone who looked like the hooded man they'd originally zoomed in on.

"No! Daniel!"

The group at the gate seemed oblivious.

She pressed the fingers of both hands over her mouth, willing them to notice what she was seeing, praying one of them would spot the enemy in time to avert disaster.

Knowing where the assailant's image on camera had originated, Daniel headed straight for that area with Dakota at heel in a short leash. Shallow drifts of snow beside the perimeter fence had preserved footprints.

He pointed at the closest prints. "Dakota. Seek."

The enormous Dane put her muzzle to the ground, then raised her head and began to strain in the direction of a shadow where beams from the floodlights didn't quite overlap.

Daniel pointed his sidearm at the same area. Just because he couldn't make out anything, didn't mean the dog was wrong. Dakota was never wrong. He'd stake his life on it, which was exactly what he was doing.

At the moment his greatest concern was that the intruder hadn't come alone. Pinpointing one danger didn't mean there were no others near enough to do damage.

"Easy," he told Dakota, keeping her close for her own protection. They edged closer to the place she'd identified.

She braced, growling. Her lip curled back. Rumbling in her deep chest gave fair warning. Something in the shadow shifted. Dakota stood on her rear legs and lunged so hard she pulled the leash out of Daniel's grip.

She was out of sight in an instant, barking and growling.

Daniel followed, two hands gripping his sidearm and every muscle in his body taut. Without a clear view of their adversary he nonetheless ordered, "Hands up!"

Dakota was no longer barking but she was growling and he could hear a scuffle. A man yelled.

Daniel closed in. His brave dog had the perp on the ground

and was holding his gun arm in her teeth while he squirmed and fought to get free.

"Drop the gun and I'll tell the dog to release you."

Their quarry cursed, fired wildly and scrambled in the snow, trying to escape.

It took Daniel only seconds to disarm the thug and make sure Dakota was uninjured. Despite Daniel's grip on the prisoner, the guy managed to wriggle away, stagger to his feet and run again. Daniel unclipped the leash from the K-9's work harness and sent her in pursuit.

While the assailant's feet rapidly pounded the ground, the Dane stretched full length and overtook him in mere moments.

The hooded man whirled, arms raised in front of his face, and absorbed the full weight and momentum of the dog as it leaped at him, drove him to the ground and stood with front feet planted on his chest.

A simple, "Dakota, out," was all it took to make her step back, panting and wagging her tail yet still concentrating on the criminal on the ground while Daniel rolled him over and cuffed his hands behind his back.

"Good girl," Daniel said. He reached for his radio and reported the capture, listening as others completed their searches without finding anyone else. Apparently, this prowler had come alone, although chances were good he had buddies either watching from a distance or keeping track via body camera. Wearing such devices had helped law officers prove themselves in the past but body cameras were a bane when used for criminal purposes.

"He has no ID on him," Daniel said after checking his pockets. "Book him for trespassing and see if we can get a name from his fingerprints or tie him to previous crimes." He led the way to the iron gates. "Make sure my team has a full report and photos of him in case they can make a match."

Lights over and around the heavy gates illuminated the

driveway like day. Placing Dakota on a Sit/Stay, he took out his phone and snapped several pictures of the man with his hood pulled off.

A quick glance toward the camera mounted on a light standard showed him that it too was recording. Good. Hopefully at least one of the images would show Aurora whether or not this shooter was the drive-by from the murder scene. If it turned out they could prove ties to the Jones/Murray group, they might be able to rule out an attack aimed at Aurora or her cousin, the ADA. Assistant District Attorneys made plenty of enemies themselves and he'd hate to discount that possibility to the detriment of that branch of law enforcement.

Incoming queries from his team drew Daniel back to the concerns of the present. He answered a group text and promised the planned video conference in ten minutes.

The gate closed behind the uniformed officers. Several patrol cars were staying in the immediate area until released, giving Daniel a modicum of peace of mind. Nothing could ever be 100 percent when you were dealing with irrational people like Brandon Jones—whose real last name was Murray, though he and his family had been living under the alias Jones. Still, having a visible police presence always helped.

That was one of the problems with life, he mused on his way back to the house. He could plan all he wanted, do everything supposedly right, and bad things could still happen. Some people blamed God for that without ever giving Him credit for the good. The truth was, people made mistakes. They made poor choices. They got themselves into trouble and either didn't know how to get out or actually liked doing wrong. That was the way he viewed the Jones brothers, particularly Brandon. Hal, may he rest in peace, may have been just as bad but he, at least, was smart enough to control some of his worst urges. That made him less dangerous than his surviving brother, Brandon. Brandon was the wild one, the unpredictable one, the loose cannon. And as such, dealing with him was akin to looking for a good time to step on a rattle-snake. There wasn't one.

Aurora heard the clicking of Dakota's nails on the hard floor outside the locked door. Nevertheless, she backed behind the desk ready to duck if necessary.

Daniel's quiet call of, "It's me," made her realize she'd been holding her breath. She released it and circled the desk, hurry-ing toward him. It was only when she realized she was ready to hug him in relief that she put on the brakes.

The abrupt stop was a bit awkward but not nearly as awk-ward as it would have been to forget herself and embrace the poor man. After all, they were colleagues, not close friends. She knew him, of course, because they both worked in and around the Plains City PD. Beyond that, they'd merely ex-changed pleasantries or talked about job-related things.

Until today, Aurora realized with a start. Something had changed today when they'd been shot at and he'd saved her. That was it. Sure. She was grateful. That made perfect sense. Thinking back, she wasn't sure she'd even thanked him, al-though she assumed she must have.

Daniel held out his hand toward her, breaking into her thoughts. "Come on."

As she naturally reached to grasp his hand, he pulled it back and motioned. "Upstairs. We need to check on Nana and Joy."

"Of course." *Of course. What did you think, that he wanted to hold your hand? Get real. This is business. All business.*

She had to hurry to keep up with him as he ran up the stairs and passed through the kitchen into the interior hallway. Nothing had been disturbed since they'd left the table so she assumed Catherine had remained with the toddler even after Daniel had called Dakota to patrol with him.

"I watched you on camera," Aurora said quietly. "Did you order a crime scene tech to look for stray bullets or brass?"

"Not yet."

"My kit is in your car. I can do it if you want."

"One thing at a time," he said, sounding gruff.

"I was just trying to help."

"Until we know whether or not you or your cousin are targets, you need to keep a low profile. Understand?"

"Of course. I stayed out of your way while you were chasing after the bad guys, didn't I?"

"It's called tracking." Huffing, he knocked on a closed door. "It's me. Dan."

The lock clicked. The door opened a crack. Aurora saw the muzzle of a gun through the narrow opening. Apparently, Catherine was well prepared to defend herself and the little one.

Daniel's arm swept up beneath the pistol to deflect it as he entered with Aurora close behind. Catherine slipped an arm around his waist and passed him the gun. "I didn't like the sound of that shot."

"Only one."

"Yes." The older woman was grinning up at him when she playfully gave his shoulder a punch. "But I didn't have my scanner so I couldn't tell what was going on. Couldn't see a blasted thing out the window either."

"Joy asleep?"

"Slept through everything," Catherine said. "I stood guard."

"Obviously. Just don't accidentally shoot me some day," Daniel teased.

Aurora's breath caught until she heard the older woman laugh and say, "Not a chance. You trained me well. The safety was on and everything."

Unshed tears of relief blurred Aurora's vision. How could these people, this odd little family, affect her this way in such a short time? She didn't have living grandparents, and with her mother gone and her father acting so awful, she did feel abandoned. Alone. Was that why she'd been so taken with the older woman and the child, not to mention the brave agent? That conclusion didn't seem logical or likely except for the fact she was unable to come up with any other reason for this odd emotional reaction.

Distancing herself by easing back into the hallway, she was hit with more uncomfortable feelings of detachment and realized that was her truth. She wasn't a part of this family or any other, and she'd be a fool to let on how much she wished for a family like the one she'd thought she'd had growing up—until her father had revealed the painful truth by trying to replace her mother almost immediately. Truth be told, any special kindness on the part of the Slaters had likely been due to her neediness as a victim.

Daniel Slater was a good man, the kind of believer who lived his faith the same way she tried to do. His actions on her behalf were merely his way of doing his job. Yes, they might seem excessive to someone who didn't treat people the same way, who didn't live life with a Christian point of view, although there were also plenty of lovely, kind folks who marched to a different drummer. So if that wasn't what set him apart in her heart and mind, what did? Given her upbringing, would she recognize a truly happy family if she saw one?

Before she had a chance to work out an answer, Catherine joined her in the hallway and took her arm. "The alarms are all set and the grounds are clear so we're going to let Joy sleep."

"Are you sure?" Aurora had unexplained misgivings.

"Positive. This place really is a fortress and Daniel says some of his people will be here soon to stand guard. You go with him while I make more coffee and get snacks ready." She smiled. "Knowing his team, they'll be hungry. They always are."

Aurora cast a glance back at the bedroom door as Daniel quietly slipped out and closed it behind him. To her relief, Dakota lay down in front of the threshold with her jowls resting on her paws.

"Oh, good."

That made him smile and warmed her heart. "I'm glad to see you appreciate my K-9 partner."

"I not only appreciate her, I'm pretty sure I remember promising her a steak for saving me when Maddie's car got shot up."

Daniel sent her a lopsided grin. "Huh. I thought I was the one who did that."

Feeling a blush rising to warm her cheeks, Aurora averted her face and said, "Okay. You two can share."

"Maybe we will, once this operation is over and things go back to some semblance of normal," he said. "In the meantime, we all need to be on our guard." He patted the grip of the gun in the holster at his waist as he led the way down the quiet hallway.

"I thought the threat was over."

He paused, turned and gave her a hard stare before he said, "Thinking like that can get you killed."

FOUR

The team video call took place in the downstairs office. While Daniel was waiting for the last of his people to connect, he showed Aurora the prowler's photo on his phone. "Is this the shooter you saw at the murder scene?"

She squinted. "Looks like him. It all happened too fast."

"I know. But he's close? Similar?"

"Yes. Same evil eyes."

"Okay. That'll do for now." He turned his attention to the video call, showing the faces of his trusted team. West Cole and Kenyon Graves, both local detectives, had called in from the police station. Tech analyst Cheyenne Chen, in a white coat, was connecting from the downtown lab the team shared with the PCPD. Calling in from home, with their backgrounds blurred, were Zach Kelcey, a deputy out of Keystone; Lucy Lopez, a Fargo patrol officer; and Liam Barringer, an agent with the FBI. Jenna Morrow, with the Cold River Sheriff's office, appeared to be in her patrol car. She was en route to South Dakota and had likely pulled over to take the call. Officer Jack Donadio appeared to be in transit.

"As you know, we've had an incident at my place," Daniel announced. "I'd appreciate it if a couple of you would assist the local PD with a night patrol over here since the guy I caught might be associated with Brandon Jones."

Jack Donadio was the first to respond. "Already on my way, Daniel. I have new info for you about Brandon."

Noticing Aurora's interest, Daniel inched aside to make room for her in front of the camera. "You all know CSI Martin. You can speak in front of her."

"Roger that." Jack kept his eyes on the road while he delivered the news. "One of my informants came to me about the murder you just investigated. Turns out, Jones got mad and killed his girlfriend, Lila Pierce, although we may have trouble proving it. But here's the good news. My guy is so disgusted with the whole Jones/Murray fiasco since Hal died he decided to come clean about their gun trafficking."

"Seriously? You believe him?"

"I do. He says another large shipment of guns is due to be moved from a warehouse in Plains City to a hiding place in Badlands National Park."

"When?"

"Tomorrow night as far as he can tell. I tried to find out if they're planning to use the same area in the Badlands where Olin and Pawners were supposed to be headed when they were taken out a few months ago, but this informant isn't sure."

"Would they be that dumb?" Daniel asked, answering himself silently in the affirmative. After all, with Brandon, the hotheaded brother, now in charge, anything was possible.

Tech analyst Cheyenne Chen piped up. "My concern is the damage to the car that Aurora borrowed from her cousin while hers is in the shop. We haven't been able to match the slugs to anything in our database."

"Her cousin is Maddie Martin, our assistant district attorney," Daniel said. "Aurora says she and her cousin look a lot alike and we wondered if that drive-by could have been a case of mistaken identity."

"Possibly," Jack said, joined by several others who concurred. "Should we head over to her place to question her?"

"No," Daniel said. "I'd like to interview her myself and take Aurora with me, tomorrow. Local PD have the ADA under surveillance and she's been informed about the threat. That'll do for now."

"Copy that. My ETA to you is five minutes. Want me to park outside or come through the gate?"

"Plains City units have the street covered. Radio or use the com link when you get here and I'll buzz you in. You can drive around back where your vehicle won't be visible. Did you bring Beau?"

"I never go anywhere without my buddy." Daniel could hear a smile in Jack's voice when he referenced his K-9 partner, a chocolate brown Lab.

"Good. I'll meet you at the back door, upper level. There's hot coffee and food in the kitchen if you want to grab some. Then run a foot patrol with Beau, pick out a good vantage point and chill. It almost took me too long to get there with Dakota when we nabbed the prowler a few minutes ago. I'll be able to rest easier with you and Beau on the job."

"All your cameras are functional?"

"Yup. You'll be a movie star by morning. It's just nicer if I don't have to stay up all night watching the monitors or listening for alarms."

"Copy." Jack cast a brief glance at the screen and teased, "You two behave yourselves, now."

Before Daniel had a chance to get mad, Aurora laughed. "We have two chaperones and a possessive dog the size of a pony. That should be enough."

Although Daniel also grinned, he was struck by the incongruity of his position. Yes, Jack had been joking but what might others think if the situation continued? Adding team members to his list of houseguests was one way to prevent rumor but they needed to be available for assignments so that wasn't a long term solution.

A safe house might be a better choice for Aurora, provided there was room available and he had time to convince her. Perhaps, once they'd visited her cousin, she'd be more amenable to the sensible suggestion.

For tonight, however, with his grandmother in the house and the area teeming with law enforcement, this arrangement would do. It would have to.

Leaving the room with all the operations visible was hard for Aurora to convince herself to do, even when Daniel tried to send her upstairs with Catherine.

"Go to the guest room," he said firmly. "Nana will show you. There's nothing more you can do down here. As soon as all my team is in position, I plan to rest too."

"What about Maddie? Are you sure she'll be all right? I mean, we could bring her here."

Daniel looked seriously troubled when he shook his head. "I'm starting to have doubts about our safety here in spite of all the alarms. It's possible moving you both to a safe house in secret would be smarter."

"There you go again," Aurora countered. "I told you how I felt about that." Her arms were folded across her chest in a clear demonstration of her choices.

"I get that. I do. Think about this. You and I may be in law enforcement but that doesn't mean we can't also be victims. You, especially. You're not armed or trained in self-defense."

"I got some training before I dropped out of police academy and changed to forensics."

"And you've been practicing?"

She had no snappy reply for that question, nor did she miss his point. "Okay. I get it. I'm an easy target. So why are the bad guys after me? I'm only doing my job."

His quick glance at his grandmother before looking toward the ceiling gave her clues. He wasn't concerned only for her welfare, he had the others to consider. One was elderly and the other was a child so neither was as capable of defending themselves as she was—and she was far from competent.

Aurora took a few slow steps toward the door and Catherine accompanied her. "All right. I am worried about Maddie so I'll give it some thought. Will that do?"

"For now," Daniel said, sounding less harsh. "I'll do my best to look after everyone and so will Dakota."

"Where is she, anyway?"

"Upstairs," Catherine answered. "She usually sleeps in front of Joy's door or next to her bed when she's home."

"I'm sure that's comforting for her." *And would be for me too, if the K-9 decided to keep me safe,* Aurora thought. She'd felt totally abandoned since her mother's death and her father's withdrawal from what was left of their family. He'd made it clear even before Mama's funeral, which he'd refused to discuss, that he was ready to put the past behind him and move on. It wasn't fair to leave all the planning to her, yet he had. And she'd managed, of course, as she always had, only this time she hadn't had her mother's wise counsel to carry her through. Then, as now, she'd been left to grieve alone, seeing clearly for the first time that the family she'd once believed was truly happy had been far from it. No wonder she'd never felt right about getting into serious relationships. She didn't really know what they were.

Those conclusions hurt. A lot. Was finding love and honesty in romance even possible? Would she recognize it if she saw it? She'd been over and over those questions in her mind until she'd finally decided, sadly, that she was a terrible judge of such things. Her father's reaction to being widowed and his rejection of her concerns about his dating so soon proved it.

Following the older woman upstairs and down the hallway to the rear of the house, Aurora was so deep in her own mind she barely noticed her surroundings. Until they passed Dakota.

As Catherine had said, the K-9 was stationed outside a bedroom door indicating Joy's room. The dog stood and waited for Catherine to open the door, then, illuminated by a dim night-light, padded quietly to the child's small bed, sniffed her for a second and laid down, as predicted.

"I'm glad she's on the job," Aurora said softly. "I'm sure you're relieved too."

"It does let me sleep more soundly," Catherine replied. "I guess it's a mother thing. We tend to listen for our children even when we're asleep."

Which was a big drawback to her decision to avoid marriage, she mused. In giving that up, she would never have children, but at least she wouldn't hurt them the way her father had hurt her—and her mother. In a way, she was glad she'd devoted so much time and energy to caring for her mother in her final years. Between that and her career, she'd had little time for outside interests and in the long run she could see that that had been a blessing in disguise.

"Here's your room," Catherine said. "I put fresh towels in the bathroom and there are some sweat suits and night things in the dresser if you want to change."

"Thanks." Aurora smiled. "I wasn't looking forward to sleeping in one of those paperlike jumpsuits we use on crime scenes. My kit's still out in Daniel's car, anyway."

"Leave it to a man to forget the necessities," Catherine said with a chuckle. "My late husband would have gone off without his head if I hadn't reminded him to take it."

A throb of compassion caused Aurora to ask, "Have you been a widow a long time?"

"Sometimes it seems like forever and other times I'll hear a noise or smell fresh-cut grass and it's as if he's still just about to walk through the door after mowing the lawn. It was his favorite chore, probably because he got to ride around the yard like a little boy on a new bike."

Tempted to mention her father, Aurora bit her tongue. This amiable woman seemed happy and well-adjusted. There was no sense bring up unhappy thoughts or conclusions. If anything, maybe watching Catherine would help her understand what was going on in her father's head, assuming he was even thinking rationally.

Her hostess paused at an open door. "I'm going to turn in too. My room is just across the hall. Once I take out my hearing aids, I won't hear much. You may have to come in and wake me in person if you need anything."

"I'm sure I'll be fine," Aurora assured her. "Thank you for everything. I know this is an imposition."

"Not at all. Our pleasure. Daniel wouldn't have asked you if there wasn't a real need. He rarely invites anyone over. If it wasn't for Joy and me, he'd probably turn into a recluse." Her smile faded and she clasped her hands as if in prayer. "I don't know what I did wrong raising his father but hopefully we can both make up for it by bringing up our Joy."

Aurora glanced in the direction of the child's room. "I'm glad she has the two of you. And Dakota. I had a dog when I was little and told him all my troubles."

"Nothing wrong with that," Catherine said. "Pets are good listeners and never gossip."

That made Aurora smile again. "Right. I hadn't thought of it that way."

"Breakfast is whenever you decide to get up. We don't live by a schedule in this house thanks to Daniel's crazy hours and a certain toddler's whims." Catherine's expression softened when she mentioned Joy again. "I figure she's doing well to get through this ordeal even though she has no idea what's happening to her mom. Daniel and I are doing our best to cushion her from the inevitable by telling her about angels and Heaven ahead of time."

"You let her do as she pleases?" She frowned slightly.

Catherine smiled. "Have you been around a lot of small children?"

"In my early teens, I was. Mom ran a day care in our home and I helped her out after school and on weekends." Now that she thought about it, perhaps those little ones were her mother's substitute for the lack of affection from her husband. "Don't children need rules?"

"Yes, and no," Catherine said. "Joy was raised like a wild child. Serena had a job for a while but once she got sick she lived in her car for months. When she heard about a drug trial taking place in Texas, she left Joy behind with a note for Dan. It was pretty confusing to the poor little thing so we cut her some slack. I think she's adjusting well, considering."

"I know some of that background. I am sorry."

"It is what it is," the older woman said. "Joy has us and Serena can be at peace about the rest of her and her child's lives because she trusts us, and God. The only thing better would be if Serena was suddenly cured." Backing into the hallway, Catherine kept her hand on the doorknob. "Do you want this open or closed?"

Aurora said, "Open," before she even thought. Access to the others and the knowledge that the faithful Great Dane was on duty just down the hall made all the difference. Isolation might be nice in some situations. Being alone tonight wasn't one of them.

Thoughts of the attacks in the street and just outside this very house made her shiver. No place was totally safe, not even a house with cameras and high fences and armed guards, although all of them added to her sense of security. Knowing that the K-9 team and officers from her very own PD were on the job was all she could ask.

Looking absently around the guest room, she noticed few feminine touches. Blinds covered the windows; the bed was unadorned and there was a single throw rug at its foot. Colors were muted and earthy. Totally masculine. That figured since Daniel had said the house had been his father's and he'd lived here alone until Catherine had moved in to look after Joy. That must have been a tough adjustment for a confirmed bachelor to make, she mused.

Beginning to give thanks that Daniel was coping with upheavals in his life, she thought of her own. "Thank you, Father, for looking after this little girl and her sick mother," Aurora whispered. "And thank you for protecting me, tonight and always." Left unsaid was the notion that she should also ask for forgiveness toward her own dad. She didn't. She couldn't. Not now. Not yet.

Truth be told, in spite of her faith, she truly didn't want to forgive him for dishonoring the memory of her dear mother and to ask for it might mean God would grant it. That was one answer to prayer she definitely did not want.

The house was silent. A soft glow from the light in the child's room shone in the hallway and for that Aurora was thankful. Not that she feared the dark, she insisted to herself. It was just nice that it wasn't pitch-black.

She turned down the bed, traded her street clothes for a warm sweatshirt and slid beneath the covers, pulling them up to her neck. She breathed deeply, slowly, trying to unwind. She prayed. She sighed. She gave herself a lecture about letting go of daily cares. And she stared at the ceiling.

Forcing her eyes to close by sheer willpower, she lay there and waited for elusive sleep. Time inched by. An owl hooted outside her window.

She was just drifting off when she thought she heard something odd. Her eyes popped open. Warmth on her cheek? Her head snapped around. Enormous teeth filled her field of vision.

Almost crying out, she took a shaky breath before she realized the sensation was dog breath and the canines belonged to the Great Dane.

Levering herself up, she leaned away from the broad dark muzzle and blinked to clear her thoughts. "Dakota?"

The K-9 gave ground.

Aurora swung her legs over the side of the bed. "What is it, girl? What do you want?"

The ropy tail began to fan the air as the huge dog circled, each turn taking her closer to the open door.

Standing, Aurora felt pulled by the dog's actions, as if she were giving her marching orders, so she followed, padding silently into the hallway on bare feet.

They went straight to Joy's room. The little girl was sitting up in bed, weeping quietly.

Aurora's heart melted. She approached, careful to let the dog lead so she didn't think the human was attacking. "Oh, honey, what's wrong?"

Joy took a shaky, shuddering breath and reached for her with both arms. "I want my mama."

FIVE

Time passed without notice as Daniel went over files about the Jones/Murray gang and their prior operations. Caches of weapons had been found buried in or near several national parks in the Dakotas. What he was looking for was a pattern. Things regarding the gun trafficking had seemed to go smoothly until Hal Murray had been killed. Now, ostensibly under the direction of his brother, Brandon, the gang actions were more random and left law enforcement guessing half the time.

They had eliminated illegal action at the pizzeria thanks to the two dead thugs who had been actively smuggling cases of guns back in the spring, had conducted a sting operation at a vineyard in South Dakota and recovered another cache of weapons, and had taken down Hal Jones/Murray who'd been the gang's mastermind. That was progress but this was November. His task force had been assigned to completely eliminate the gun trafficking ring and still had plenty of work to do.

While he had Joy and Serena to worry about, Daniel added with a shake of his head. If it wasn't one thing, it was another. Almost every member of his team had personal problems to distract them. But that was just life, wasn't it? Nobody escaped worldly troubles no matter how secluded or perfect a life they tried to lead. Add a law enforcement career to that and you had a guaranteed headache. Period.

He pushed away from the console, paused to check the monitors showing the exterior grounds, then nodded, pleased. Jack Donadio and Beau were on the job at the rear of the house and a Plains City police car was parked in the street, purposely visible. The only thing better would be that imaginary moat Aurora had teased him about.

Leaving the lower level, he silently climbed the stairs.

Light shone dimly from Joy's bedroom, as always, making it easy to check on her in passing or if she awoke in the night. They had come to the conclusion that she sometimes had disturbing dreams because she'd been known to begin crying and call for him or his grandmother for no apparent reason.

An otherwise silent house accentuated every little sound so Daniel lightened his footsteps. Dakota would hear him coming, of course. That was a given. He simply didn't want to awaken the toddler or either of the sleeping women.

A soft feminine tone of voice reached his ears and he stopped. Catherine? No. It didn't sound like her. And since the person was speaking in sentences, that ruled out little Joy, although her grasp of language improved daily.

Daniel eased closer, stopping beside Joy's doorway so he could listen without being seen. Aurora was apparently reading a story. Or was she?

"That's right," the gentle voice said. "The princess was named Joy, just like you, and she was very happy to live in the pretty castle where she had her own room just like this one and everybody loved her very much."

His heart clenched. Aurora was making up a fairy tale and using his niece's name for the heroine. It was genius. And it touched him deeply.

"Where's my horsey?" the child asked, sounding enrapt.

"Ah, yes, you need a pony," Aurora said. "Let me see. I know. The pony is pretending to be a big lovable tan dog with brown eyes and black on her face around her nose and ears."

"Doh-dah!"

"Yes, Dakota. Can you say, Dah?"

"Da."

"Co?"

"Co."

"Tah?"

"Dah," Joy said, clapping her chubby hands. "Doh-dah."

Daniel heard Aurora laugh lightly. "That's right. Our sweet friend, Dakota."

"I ride Doh-dah."

"I heard. You need to be sure it's okay with Uncle Daniel before you do that though. You don't want to hurt her. You love her, right?"

"Uh-huh. Lub her."

"And you love Uncle Daniel and Grandma Catherine too."

"Nana has cookies."

"That's wonderful. Princesses like Joy love cookies, don't they?"

"Uh-huh."

Daniel silently took a step into the doorway and watched. Joy was cuddled up next to Aurora with a blanket wrapped around them both. Soft rays from the night-light illuminated the woman's long blond hair from behind, making it glow as if an aura surrounded her and the child. He didn't think he'd ever seen a sight so beautiful, so ethereal.

Aurora's long lashes lifted and she made eye contact with him before continuing. "Princess Joy has lots of people who love her. She's a very blessed little girl."

Joy raised her face to Aurora's. "What's best?"

"Blessed? Well, blessed is like when good things happen to us and we thank Jesus for them because we know He loves us too and wants us to be happy."

"Mama loves Jesus," Joy said sobering. "Mama's sick."

"Yes, I know, honey. That's sad. I'm sorry."

Daniel fought the moisture pooling in his eyes, yet couldn't make himself look away. He and Catherine had tried to explain Serena's illness to Joy but up until now they hadn't been sure she'd understood any of it.

"Will Jesus make her better?"

That was the longest sentence Daniel had ever heard the child construct and he was awed. All his prayers for Serena had apparently fallen on deaf ears.

"Sometimes that happens," Aurora said, visibly pulling the child closer, "and sometimes our mamas go home to Heaven to be with Jesus. That's what my mama did."

"Awww." Joy leaned against Aurora and patted her arm.

"It's okay," she assured the toddler. "My mama loved Jesus too. I know she's happy being with Him in Heaven."

"My mama too?" The question was so faint Daniel could barely hear it and it broke his heart for his innocent niece.

"I think maybe," Aurora said, once again meeting his gaze. "That means she won't be sick or hurt anymore."

"Okay," Joy said, brightening. "Tell me a story again."

And just like that the life lesson was over. Joy had accepted reality in a simple way adults found impossible. Part of him was glad that Aurora had presented the facts of her faith with such gentle tact while another part of him was jealous that he and others had failed to succeed.

So it often was with God's divine plans, he concluded. His prayers for the right words to comfort the child had been answered in a way beyond his imaginings. Where he had wanted to impart understanding, the Lord had sent someone else instead. Someone with an open heart who had the right words at the right time. There was no way he could fault the result since it directly accomplished the goal he'd prayed for.

With Joy's concentration on Aurora, he took the chance she

wouldn't notice when he signaled that he was going to go on to his room and sleep. Dakota watched, of course, so he also held out a flat palm to instruct the dog to stay where she was.

Aurora nodded, sniffling, then looked away. He was in no better shape. The moment he turned to go and knew his face was hidden, tears crested his lower lashes and began to run down his beard-stubbled cheeks.

He'd been raised by his late father to believe real men never wept. Perhaps men with hard hearts who led unfaithful lives like his father's didn't. Denying his daughter, Serena, was a prime example of his father's closed heart and mind.

Daniel swiped at his face, filled with disgust for his dad yet awash with emotions of compassion and gratefulness for what he'd just observed. He couldn't go back in time and correct the mistakes of others but he could do his best to make a good life for Joy and see that Serena had the kindest place in which to spend her final days and hours, however many that might be.

An unspoken prayer of thanks bloomed in his thoughts. As usual, the Lord had used events that had seemed bad and turned the results to good by causing him to bring that extraordinary young woman into his home to offer solace just when Joy needed her. It shouldn't have surprised him, yet it did.

The irony of his reasoning made him snort a wry chuckle. Was he so hardheaded that God had to let somebody shoot at him to make a point? He shook his head derisively. Could be.

Aurora had not intended to remain with Joy but the warm bed, the soft comforter and the snoring dog on the floor next to them had apparently lulled her to sleep.

She awoke slowly, taking a moment to realize where she was and to ease her arm from around the toddler. Sunlight was peeking in through a gap in the curtains and she thought she could hear activity in a distant part of the house. She inhaled. *Coffee?*

Sliding cautiously out of bed, she stood and looked down at the sleeping child. Dakota also stood and stretched, taking up half the space next to the bed before looking to her and walking off, apparently deciding it was time for the humans to take over babysitting.

Joy stirred. Her butterfly lashes fluttered. When she looked up and saw Aurora, she grinned, then sobered. "I miss my mama."

"I know you do, sweetheart." She held out her hand and the tiny fingers grasped it. "Come on. Let's get you dressed so you can go see Uncle Daniel and your nana."

"Where's Doh-dah?"

"Dakota left because it was time for us to get up. Come on. I'll help you."

"Okay."

The child's trust was so complete it almost made Aurora weep again. She had to quit doing that or poor Joy was going to think she was supposed to be sad too. Recalling the explanation she'd given the night before about going to Heaven, Aurora sighed. Those words had come so easily she was still shocked. The times when things like that happened to her were rare, yet strengthened her faith immeasurably. In trying to comfort and bless the innocent little girl, she, herself, had been blessed beyond measure.

It was almost enough to make a person forget she had potentially been the target of assassins mere hours ago.

A sense of maternal responsibility rose in Aurora's heart as she tended to Joy's morning routine. This little one needed protecting beyond her personal capabilities. Therefore, she must step up and assist Daniel however she could. No wonder he was so cautious, so determined to make up for the failings of others. She got that. If she could have somehow imparted peace to her own father, she would have. But that was another story, wasn't it?

One problem at a time, Aurora told herself. She straightened after brushing the child's fine blond hair and smiled. "There. All done. Ready for breakfast, honey?"

"Uh-huh." Joy smoothed the cartoon T-shirt she'd chosen to wear. "I look like a princess, huh."

"Yes, you look beautiful."

"Yeah."

"The polite thing to say would be thank you."

"Okay." She giggled behind her hand. "Tank you."

"You're very welcome, princess. Come on. Let's go get something to eat. I'm starving."

As they left the child's room together, Joy reached up and clasped one of Aurora's fingers as if it was the most natural thing in the world, and the show of childish trust was so touching it almost brought her to tears. This innocent little one counted on the adults in her life to keep her safe when their own lives were in turmoil. Her mother was dying and would soon be gone, her uncle was embroiled in a manhunt that had already caused members of his team to be wounded and had created a vendetta against law enforcement. And she—Aurora tensed—even she had been shot at. It was as if the people who cared for Joy were dancing on a knife-edge with no safety net and all she could do was pray and hope.

She swallowed hard. It was a lot easier to claim that she trusted God fully when things were peaceful, wasn't it?

SIX

Daniel had been relating the latest developments in the gun trafficking case to Jack over coffee in the kitchen. He greeted Aurora and Joy with a smile. "Good morning, ladies." He gestured. "You know Jack Donadio, don't you, Aurora?"

"Yes. I hope you and Beau didn't get too cold last night."

"We kept each other warm," Jack quipped. He raised his mug. "Coffee?"

"I'll get it." Daniel was already on his feet. "Nana will look after our little friend."

"I'm a princess," Joy said, striking a pose with her hands on her hips.

That made everyone laugh. Daniel was grinning broadly. "So I heard." He looked to Aurora. "That was quite a story you were telling her last night."

"How much of it did you overhear?"

"It doesn't matter. What I did hear was spot on. Very helpful if you know what I mean."

"Spiritually?"

"Yes." He indicated Catherine where she was offering food to the toddler now perched in a high chair and she nodded. "We both appreciate it." Aurora was smiling wistfully and Daniel couldn't help remembering how beautiful she had looked the night before.

"Join us," he said, bringing a mug of hot coffee to the table for her. "We were just discussing plans for the day."

"Do they include me?" she asked.

Daniel nodded. "Yes. We're going to the courthouse to visit your cousin Maddie and see if we can figure out who made Swiss cheese out of her car."

"I'm glad you told her. Was she very upset?"

Because of the way Aurora was gripping the mug in both hands and frowning, he reassured her. "She understands it wasn't your fault."

"That's a relief."

He chuckled. "We thought it would be. There was a guard on her house all night and we've added plainclothes officers to the staff at the courthouse, just in case. She's promised to go over her recent prosecutions and try to come up with names of possible suspects."

"She and I do kind of look alike. Do you actually think the shooter mistook me for Maddie?"

The truth seemed appropriate. "No, I don't. However, there have also been threats against me and my team. You may have been standing next to the target. Me."

Pensive, Aurora stared into her steaming coffee for a moment before agreeing. "I can see that, although the shooter didn't put holes in your SUV."

"They may have known it's reinforced steel with bullet-proof glass."

"Or they were a lousy shot. Did your people get any info out of the guy you grabbed last night?"

"Nope. Not a whisper."

Jack piped up. "We do think he's associated with Brandon Jones/Murray."

"Ah. Maybe it wasn't about me or Maddie. It would be nice to know for sure."

"Which is why we'll meet with her this morning," Daniel

offered. "Grab a bite to eat and get changed while Jack and I do a last sweep of the grounds. We'll leave in an hour." Noting her worried glance at the toddler and Catherine, he added, "Jack will stay here while we're gone and hold down the fort."

At this, Aurora cracked a smile. "You mean man the turrets in this castle, don't you? After all, there is a princess in residence."

"Me!" echoed from the high chair and little arms waved with delight.

"That's right," Daniel said. "Princess Joy. We can't forget that. I know your mama will be glad to hear all about it when we go see her this afternoon."

"Yeah!" The little hands clapped, scattering bits of dry cereal onto the floor where Dakota faithfully scooped up each crumb.

"How is Serena today?" Aurora asked aside.

Sobering, Daniel shook his head and leaned closer to speak privately. "No change." Hospice nurses had numbered Serena's days down to a few. Part of him wanted her to remain for Joy's sake and part of him hoped she'd pass peacefully. Some people thought it was terrible to think such thoughts but he too trusted the teachings of his Christian faith for Serena's future. Without that, he'd have been devastated. God had reunited him with his half sister in time to help her and assume the responsibility for her daughter. Now that Serena knew Joy would always have a stable home with him, she'd told him she was ready to go. More than that, he couldn't ask for.

"I'm sorry. Should you see her this morning instead of waiting?"

"No. She's sedated. Her nurses have arranged to let her wake up to visit at two. We'll go then."

Nodding, Aurora nibbled at a strip of bacon and ate a few bites of scrambled egg before she pushed away from the table.

"I'll go put on my regular clothes. I'd like to stop by my apartment and pick up a few things too, if we can."

"I'll have Officer Jenna Morrow do that for you. Makes sense to send a woman."

Aurora blushed. "You've got that right. Thanks."

From the high chair came a piercing echo, "Tank *you*."

Laughing lightly, Aurora blushed more. "Right. Thank you, Agent Slater."

He stood and bowed with a broad sweep of his arm as if they were acting in an Elizabethan drama. "A pleasure, m'lady. Anything for a member of our princess's court."

It pleased him to note the high color in Aurora's pale cheeks as she turned to leave. Her hair and eyes were a lot like Joy's and also reminded him of his half sister, although Serena's hair was now gone because of the harsh chemo treatments. Thankfully, Joy never seemed to notice. She'd certainly never asked about it. Maybe that was just how children were. They accepted things without thinking them to death the way adults did.

Like going to Heaven, he added to himself. Joy had immediately seen the beauty Aurora described and stopped fretting about it. Maybe that was why Jesus had said believers needed to "come as a child." It made sense. Children's hearts were pure enough to take in the wonders of eternity without spoiling the picture with their versions of reality. Perhaps children were given a special insight that adults somehow lost as they lived life.

There were times, like when he visited his ailing half sister, when he dearly wished he didn't know how badly their father had treated her and her late mother, not to mention his own mom. If there was one person he was determined to never emulate, it was that hard-hearted, selfish man. The only good thing Daniel could see that had come out of his father's sins was Serena and the sweet little girl with big blue eyes and hair

like spun gold who was currently pitching pieces of her breakfast at Dakota and laughing as the dog tried to catch them.

He would always be there for her, he vowed. Always.

A tiny voice inside reminded him of the dangers of his chosen career and he acknowledged that truth. Would he give up
a job he loved and was good at for the sake of the little girl's
happiness? If it came to that he thought he could do so. In the
meantime, he intended to rely on his DGTF team to get him
through the rough patches.

An image of Aurora as a beautiful bride coming toward
him as he stood at an altar flashed into his mind. *No. Not her.*
And certainly not now. He didn't need the distractions of a
romance pulling his thoughts from his job and weakening his
focus. The longer the gun traffickers were in operation the
more innocent civilians would die and it was up to him to give
full attention to leading his team. They were all superb officers with amazing K-9 partners but even they needed proper
direction and it was his job to provide it.

Besides, he and Catherine were providing all the love and
support the soon-to-be orphan needed. His gut clenched. It
was going to be tough losing his sister so soon after finding
out he had one at all but he'd cope. He owed it to the people
his father had hurt to make up for the man's perfidy. It was
the least he could do.

And while he was at it, he had a gun trafficking operation
to break up and murders to solve.

Aurora was both surprised and impressed when she was
led into the immense garage through a secret side entrance
and driven out via a rear exit camouflaged by bushes and a
cut into the hill on which the house was built.

"Well, it's almost a moat," she remarked. "I can't believe
all the special features of your home."

"I told you. My father needed to take precautions because

of the twisted life he led. I was going to sell the place when I first inherited it. Now I'm glad I didn't."

"So, am I. It has to be safer than those houses you tried to get me to move into."

She started to scowl when he disagreed with her. "Not necessarily. Remember what happened last night."

"You saw the prowler coming because of your cameras."

"Yes, but he found me, found us, easily. That's a problem if that guy is part of the gang we've been tracking."

Daniel glanced over at her and she quickly looked away, hoping he hadn't noticed her studying his profile. There was something unusually compelling about this man, this business-like federal agent who had taken in a waif and was helping a sister he'd only recently met. And Catherine. What a lovely older lady she was. So wise and gentle. Given the familial connection, it was easy to assume Daniel possessed those same qualities in spite of his masculinity and aura of command.

As she watched him drive, she noticed how often he checked the mirrors and kept track of traffic behind them as well as to the front and sides. Nothing missed his scrutiny. That was comforting to see.

They were approaching downtown Plains City with its quaint Western charm interspersed with modern businesses like the pizzeria. "We should treat Catherine and Joy to pizza one of these nights."

"Not from that place," Daniel said quickly. "I'm not exactly welcome there and I wouldn't trust the food."

"Wow. What did they do, add anchovies?"

An arch of his brows was all the explanation she got. That was enough to remind her of an operation back in the spring involving a couple of men who had worked out of the restaurant and ended up dead.

Aurora nodded. "Sorry. That's right. I'd forgotten."

"Catherine makes better pizza anyway," he said. "I called

the DA's office and your cousin is off today so I figured we'd stop by her condo if that's all right with you."

"Fine." Aurora was nodding and thinking of the austere office where Maddie worked. Catching her at home would be better and more private too.

"You're familiar with her apartment building?"

"I've been there visiting. We don't get together often though. My family was never close and after Mom died... Well, you get the idea."

"You don't see your dad often?"

She wanted to curl up in a ball and disappear. Instead, she crossed her arms and shook her head. "Never, if I can help it."

Hoping that Daniel would change the subject she was disappointed when he asked, "Do you suppose he's just really lonely?"

"Of course he is. So am I. But you don't see me adopting a new mom, do you?"

"Oh, I don't know. You seemed to get along well with my nana."

"She's easy to like. So what?"

"Nothing. I get it," Daniel said. "If my father was still alive, I doubt I'd be speaking to him either."

Aurora sighed. "We're a pair, aren't we?"

"Not good examples of forgiveness, if that's what you mean."

"I'm not ready," she said flatly. "Are you?"

Chuckling under his breath, he gave her a lopsided smile. "How did we get off on this subject anyway?"

"I don't know."

"Me either. Let's lighten the mood and talk shop."

"Sure. Nothing like theft and smuggling and an occasional murder to liven up a conversation." Aurora couldn't help returning his smile. "At least we have one informant who confirmed Brandon Jones/Murray killed his poor girlfriend. That's going to be a big help."

"Only if we can come up with hard evidence." He leaned and pointed at a nondescript two-story brick building to his right. "Is that your cousin's place?"

"Yes. She has a covered parking spot around back."

Daniel continued to smile. "Well, it won't have her car in it because it's still impounded so we may as well park there."

She made a face at him. "Don't remind me," she said as they got out of the car and he released Dakota.

The impressive dog was dressed for work in her heavy vest and identifying harness and she stood as if ready to take on any and all threats.

Aurora shuddered. Investigating cases as a CSI was far different than being so close to the action. Or, worse, feeling like a target.

Hurrying ahead, she punched in the code for the outer door and entered the brick building. Maddie's unit was on the third floor, rear, with a spectacular view of the Black Hills range. Sunsets lit it up and colored the early snow like a magnificent aurora, something Maddie like to kid her about because of her unusual name.

"Elevators are over here," she said, taking the lead.

"Staircases?" Daniel asked, clearly task-oriented, as was his K-9.

"There and there." She pointed.

He joined her at the elevator. The change in his working persona was so distinct it made her anxious.

Dakota boarded the elevator without a qualm and stood tall at Daniel's side. The ride was over in seconds. As the doors slid open and she prepared to step out, the agent stopped her.

"We'll go first," he said. "Left or right?"

"Right."

"Stay close."

"Nobody followed us did they?"

"Not that I saw. Standard procedure for entering unknown areas is to use the dog. That's what she's here for."

To Aurora's relief, the distance to Maddie's apartment was short. She knocked. No one answered so she called, "Mads? You home?"

Still no answer. Casting a concerned look at Dan, she reached into a thin recess behind the jamb and pulled out a key. "Safer than leaving it under a mat or a flowerpot," she said, unlocking the door.

Again, Daniel stopped her with an extended arm before she could enter, so she stepped aside for him. Dakota entered slowly, nose in the air, hackles showing slightly above the vest where it crossed her shoulders by her neck.

Ears pricking forward, she stopped. Growled. Stiffened.

Daniel reached for the sidearm holstered beneath his jacket.

Aurora froze, afraid to breathe, let alone move or speak.

He signaled her to duck behind a group of white sofas arranged in an L to facilitate intimate conversations. When she didn't move immediately, he turned and ordered, "Get down," without waiting to see if she obeyed.

Then he and Dakota were gone and she was all alone in the silent living room, listening to the sound of her heart pounding in her ears and her breath shuddering as she tried to quiet it.

Time stopped.

Dakota's sharp bark rattled the windows.

There was a thud. Sounds of a scuffle.

Then a gunshot. Just one.

And silence.

SEVEN

Daniel had been in a crouch thanks to Dakota's alert and the bullet zinged harmlessly over his head. He heard it impact the wall. An acrid odor of gunpowder filled the small bedroom as a whiff of smoke from the shot lingered.

He'd commanded his K-9 to hit the floor and kept her there for her own safety while he assessed the situation. The gunman had fired while hiding inside a closet and as far as he could tell was still there. Bracing, he started to rise to peer over the bed.

Something loomed on his right. Dakota pivoted as best she could without breaking orders. A shoulder rammed into Daniel, driving him to the floor. Hard.

Dakota lunged and snapped, barely missing the thug's ankle as it passed. A harsh voice cursed. Daniel scrambled to his knees preparing to rise when a second shot rang out. He could tell the caliber of this gun was larger than those that had been used against them previously. Larger and more deadly. Whoever had fired at him was on the move toward the exit. Toward Aurora.

"Stay down!" he shouted, hoping and praying she'd listen and take heed.

Shadows dressed in dark clothing filled the doorway, then were gone. He gave chase as far as the hallway, keeping his K-9 at his side rather than sending her after the assailants alone and making her an easy target.

Using his body and Dakota's to block the doorway, he reported to headquarters. "Yes, Agent Slater... That's right... In ADA Martin's apartment... No, I don't know where she is. I'll stay in control of the scene until local PD arrive. Then we're going to the courthouse to try to find out who might be involved in shooting up Martin's car and breaking into her condo."

He noted Aurora peeking over the back of the sofa and signaled to her to wait as he continued speaking into his radio. "Copy. ETA five."

With one arm extended toward Aurora, he motioned for her to join him.

She was hesitant. "Are you sure they're gone?"

"Dakota tells me everyone left and she's never wrong."

"Oh, good." The slump of her shoulders showed how affected she was by the frightening events. "What about Maddie? She was supposed to be home. You don't think..."

Left unsaid was the same question Daniel had asked himself as soon as he'd realized there were unknown people in the apartment. He gestured at Aurora. "Grab your cell and give her a call at the office. Who knows. She may have decided to go to work after all."

"If she did go in on her day off, I'll give credit to God," Aurora said. Although her hands were trembling, she managed to punch up the listing and dial Maddie's private line. Daniel could tell by the astonishment in her expression that she'd made the connection. "Maddie, it's me! We came by your place and somebody shot at us."

The reply was almost loud enough to understand. "Hang on. I want Agent Slater to hear this too." She pushed a button, then said, "Okay. Go ahead. You're on speaker."

"What are you doing over there? And why is the ATF with you? I haven't tried any smuggling cases lately."

"It's complicated," Aurora said. She thrust the phone at him. "You tell her."

"Your possible involvement goes back to the bullet holes in your car, ma'am," Daniel said. "Have you been able to recall anyone else who may have a grudge against you?"

"There's quite a list, actually," Maddie said. "Is Aurora all right? She sounds scared silly."

"I'll look after her. Right now we're trying to sort out the members of the Jones/Murray organization from all the other low-life thugs in Plains City. Like you said. It's a long list."

"There is one old case in particular," Maddie said. "I'll send over the files on Kyra Fellowes and her boyfriend, Tim. They gave me some grief after Kyra's drug conviction about three years ago and she was recently released on probation. Still, it's a big jump to go from selling drugs to attempted murder."

Daniel had to agree with her there. If anything, most criminals went out of their way to keep a low profile. "Were either of them ever linked to Brandon or Hal Jones, aka Murray?"

"Not that I know of but it's been years. That might be a lead worth checking. It's possible Kyra made some new friends while she was serving time." She paused. "Plus, we're about to start a high-profile murder trial. Derek Carlson has been charged with the murder of his wife."

"That prominent South Dakota businessman? I remember the arrest. You're prosecuting?"

"We are, Maddie said. "I'm looking forward to seeing justice done."

"Right." Sirens in the street echoed through the open hallway. "Sounds like the PCPD has arrived here. We'll go back to the station. You stay at the courthouse and don't take any chances until we find out who and what we're up against." Maddie's laugh sounded to him like Aurora's and made him smile.

"Good advice," Aurora drawled. "I'm getting a personal

tutorial on staying safe. See you later." Ending the call, she looked to Daniel. "Well?"

"Well what?"

"I think we're long past plan B or C. What's next?"

"Like I told your cousin, we'll go back to the station. I have reports to write and I want to check on the tips Maddie just gave us."

"Do you really think it's two separate cases?"

"That makes as much sense as thinking the shootings are linked. We know Brandon killed Lila but we don't know if that's connected to the times you've come under fire."

"Or who was hiding in Maddie's condo just now. I'm afraid for her too."

"I've been giving that some thought," Daniel said. "The smartest move would be to separate any of the people who have apparently been targeted and place them in safe houses."

"I told you how I felt about taking up space intended for helpless victims."

"Yes, you did. And I took you to my house, which was then attacked by the gunman we took into custody. Not my most lucid decision."

"You think he was after me?"

"Beats me. The only one who knows is the guy in custody and he immediately asked for a lawyer so we haven't been able to get anything out of him."

She opened her mouth, probably intending to argue. Rather than do so, he put Dakota on a Sit/Stay next to the doorway and stepped forward to greet the arriving police officers.

"Stand down. The fun's over," Daniel told them, waving his hands for emphasis. "The shooters got away. I stayed to turn the crime scene over to you and your people."

The officers shook hands and exchanged brief pleasant-ries before they entered the empty apartment with him. In moments, he'd identified the points of impact of the bullets fired and been reassured that the apartment's owner would be properly looked after.

"We can go," he said, rejoining Aurora and his K-9. "Dakota, Heel."

"That's it? What about poor Maddie? She can't safely come home, can she?"

"I'd prefer she didn't," he said flatly as he led the way to the elevator. "Lorelei Danvers is the US marshal who arranged for your old teacher to be moved to a secret location. She can handle any changes that need to be made for your cousin too, although I assume she'll want to retain her name and job in spite of threats, which will create a whole new set of problems. If every law enforcement professional hid when a threat was made, we wouldn't have anyone left."

"What about Joy and Catherine? Jack can't stay with them 24/7. He has a job to do with your team."

"That's right, he does. We all do."

She arched an eyebrow at him. "Meaning?"

"Meaning, fun and games are over. This is no longer up for discussion. You will go to a safe house as soon as I can make proper arrangements.

"With Maddie? I'd actually like that."

"Not if I can help it. Assuming the threats to her aren't connected to the ones involving you, we'd be compounding the problem by putting you together."

"But…"

"No buts," he said firmly, crossing his arms and wishing he didn't have to be so inflexible.

When Aurora mimicked his stubborn pose, he figured she was far from finished arguing with him. He was right.

"At least ask Maddie to meet us at the station. That should be safe enough and it's close to the courthouse."

"Any particular reason?" He stepped onto the elevator with his dog and the hardheaded CSI.

"I'd like to see her, if you must know. It's been a lousy couple of days and I need a friend."

That took him aback. It was an honest admission—she felt vulnerable. "I thought you and I were friends," he teased.

"You're an ATF agent in charge of a team of specialists. I'm just a tech."

"Since when has rank made a difference?" Daniel asked.

The pathos in her glance when she made eye contact hit him like a punch in the gut. She viewed him as an authority figure because that was exactly the vibe he'd been giving off, which was as it should be under normal circumstances. But these weren't normal events, were they? Their lives had been threatened repeatedly and he needed to let Aurora know she could count on him in a personal way as well as formally.

That was a wall he wasn't sure he wanted to breach, not now, not ever, and yet his heart went out to the young woman. She'd recently lost her mother and was estranged from her father. Little wonder she wanted to spend time with her cousin, particularly if Maddie was the only remaining member of her immediate family.

Finding the right words to comfort would not only be difficult, but make it hard to backtrack if he was misunderstood.

Instead, he merely took a step closer, opened his arms and said, "Come here."

She turned to face him.

"Friends," he said tenderly.

In a heartbeat, she was in his embrace and hugging him as if she'd never let go. Daniel was stunned. He'd handed out hugs to team members before but those had felt nothing like this. Not even close. Holding this woman was so special he had no words, no rational thoughts. When had she become so important to him? he wondered. When had his emotions crossed the line that he was just now outwardly expressing?

Loosening his hold a bit, he felt Aurora's arms slacken too.

Part of him insisted he apologize and step away. A stronger part argued vehemently against it.

She leaned back enough to raise her face to his. There were tears in her eyes, her cheeks were damp and her lips were slightly parted. She didn't speak or try to explain. She didn't have to. It was evident to Daniel that she was feeling their amazing connection the same way he was. At least he hoped she was, because he was sorely tempted to kiss her.

At the last instant, he regained enough sensibility to hold back and place the gentle kiss on her forehead.

The elevator doors opened. They jumped apart. Daniel wasn't positive whether or not he was glad, but judging by the way Aurora had immediately withdrawn, he was pretty sure she was.

Striding out the ground floor exit ahead of Daniel and Dakota, Aurora was so disoriented she figured she was doing well to simply put one foot in front of the other. What had just happened? Had she actually made a pass at the agent who was merely there to protect her? It sure felt like it.

Warmth flooded her cheeks so she kept her face averted. *Mercy*! as Mama would have said. What was wrong with her? She practically begged him to hug her and when he did, she reacted as if they were lovers and he wanted to kiss her. How embarrassing. And how unprofessional. They were colleagues, even though her job didn't fall directly under his auspices. Being a crime scene tech put her in a different category than true law enforcement and she wasn't the only one who considered her position far below that of a supervisor of any rank.

Whether to apologize or try to overlook her error kept whirling through her brain. If he hadn't meant anything by the tenderness, if it was as casual as it would be with anyone, talking about it would make things worse. If, however, Daniel had been as emotionally invested in their embrace as she'd been, it was a subject best broached ASAP.

Circling his SUV, Aurora climbed into the passenger side and busied herself fastening the seat belt while he loaded Dakota from the rear. As soon as he started the engine, she began rubbing her hands together in front of the vent again.

Daniel reached over and grasped both her hands. "You're shaking."

"I'm okay."

"I know." A gentle tone that she was beginning to recognize softened his voice. Letting go, he cleared his throat. "I'm sorry if…"

"Me too," she broke in.

"We should probably forget it happened."

"Oh, yeah. Definitely," she said. Only she wouldn't. She couldn't. This was the perfect time to open up and confess the feelings she was starting to have for him. It was also more involvement than he'd alluded to with his effort to apologize. If he'd shared her growing fondness, he surely wouldn't have said he was sorry.

And so Aurora leaned back in the seat, folded her hands in her lap and kept silent. She'd never had to fight having undue affection for any of the police officers or other PCPD staff. This was new. Unsettling and a little frightening if she allowed herself to imagine forming a relationship with Daniel Slater. Yes, he was handsome and had all the other good attributes she admired in a man, but she was never going to settle down the way her parents had. Too many marriages, sadly including theirs, ended unhappily. He was apparently happy single and so was she. Therefore, encouraging romance was the last thing she wanted to do.

But, oh, it had felt good to be held. To be cared for if only for a moment. People in her church gave hugs and for that she was always grateful, but this hug, this specific closeness, was different. Better. Special and protective without being constrictive or dominating the way it felt when her father had tried to hug her once after they'd quarreled about his new lifestyle.

So, this hug can be filed away with my nice memories and never needs to be repeated. That was logical. Sensible. Appropriate. She made a face of personal derision. It was all those things. What she needed to do now was convince herself that the close encounter in the elevator with the senior agent was a fluke.

And keep from blushing every time she saw him. Too bad it wasn't still summer when she could have blamed her high color on a sunburn. Truth to tell, she had enough problems just dodging real bullets without adding having to dodge *emotional* ones.

EIGHT

The police station was as busy as ever. Parking in the rear, Daniel punched in the entrance code and led Dakota and the pretty CSI through a back door. His team's office space was on an upper floor.

"Do you need to check in or anything?" he asked Aurora.

"I suppose I should. I'd like to be there when we do the ballistics on the slugs from Maddie's apartment and see if they match the ones from her car. Our people are good, I just want to hurry the process."

"Okay. If you get finished before I do, come and find me."

"In other words, don't go anywhere without you?"

Her cynical tone made him choose a lighthearted reply. "I have orders to bring you back with me tonight. Joy insisted."

To his relief, Aurora began to smile. "For a minute there, I thought you were going to blame Dakota."

"Oh, she agrees. She's just not as good with words as the *princess*. Thank you for that, by the way. Joy needed to feel special."

"She is special."

"No argument there." Starting to step away, he looked back over his shoulder. "I know you're perfectly safe here in the station but please check with me from time to time, will you? I'm not asking for a minute-by-minute schedule. I'd just be grateful if you'd keep in touch."

With a growing smile, Aurora teased, "And don't leave town?"

Daniel laughed. "Right. Something like that."

He hated to let her out of his sight even in such a secure environment, which made little or no sense when he thought about it. Nobody had assigned him to guard the young CSI and when he considered his growing feelings about her, he could see a problem in the offing. It would be easy enough to hand her off to another member of his team or even speak to the police chief and have her immediately placed in protective custody. That's what he should do, he told himself. What he was going to do, however, was keep her with him for as long as possible because something in his gut kept telling him she'd be better off if he did.

Logic had little to do with it, he realized with a start. He was going to keep a personal eye on Aurora Martin because he wanted to. He needed to. It was as if he'd been assigned to care for her from the moment he'd saved her life at the murder scene.

The way she'd comforted Joy was another reason he wanted her near. He and Catherine had worked with the toddler for months before gaining the kind of trust Aurora had received in the space of mere hours. Of course, she was closer to Serena's age and perhaps their hair was similar enough to remind Joy of her mother. Which reminded him.

Rather than use the phone in his office, he pulled out his cell to call Catherine. Instead of hello, she answered with, "What's wrong?"

"Nothing," Daniel assured her. "I was just thinking of Serena and wanted to make sure you didn't mind my going with you and Joy to visit her today. The last time I spoke with hospice they said her time was short."

"Absolutely. Meet us there a little after two." There was a hesitation.

"And?" Daniel asked.

"And, I think you should bring our friend, Aurora. I know Joy would like it and I think it would be good for her to meet your sister."

Realizing that Catherine wouldn't know about the disturbance at Maddie's, he kept his reply simple. "Until we get more answers about everything that's been happening I plan to keep a close eye on Aurora."

"I'm glad," Catherine said. Daniel could tell by the tenderness in her voice that she too liked the pretty CSI.

"Yeah, well, it's my job."

"I love you," Catherine said. "And I know what you've always said about settling down and starting a family, but..."

"I have a family. Ready-made," he said flatly. "Joy will be my daughter as soon as I can legally adopt her and you're the maternal influence in her life. That's all I need."

His grandmother's sigh was loud enough to hear over the phone. "See you at two, then," she said, "Bye, dear."

Ending the call, he pocketed his phone, removed his coat, circled his desk and sat down, opening the folder at the top of a pile. It was a printout of the Kyra Fellowes case, Maddie Martin's top suspect. Since the woman had recently been paroled there was a possibility she, or her boyfriend from before conviction, had surfaced to carry out the threats they'd made three years before. A check with her parole officer was called for, as was a trace on her current whereabouts. He kept reading, making notes.

A knock on his door an hour later startled him. "Come in."

The face that peeked around the side of the door at him was smiling and, seeing who it was, he began to grin. "That didn't take long. Was there a match on the bullets?"

Entering the office, Aurora shook her head as she dropped her coat on a chair. She'd changed from jeans and a T-shirt to dark slacks and a polo with the PCPD logo on one shoulder.

It didn't escape his notice that she looked wonderful no matter what she wore. "Nope. No matches. Those guys must have more guns than an army."

"Ghost guns are part of their cache," Daniel said.

"The ones where they order separate parts and make them up themselves?"

"Right. With no serial numbers. Impossible to trace."

"Just as lethal though," Aurora said. He thought he saw her shiver.

Daniel stood and circled the desk. He knew he could have told her to have a seat and wait for him to finish his reading but it was suddenly important to place himself nearer to her. Dakota got up from her cozy spot next to a file cabinet and followed.

"I was considering asking your cousin to meet us for lunch if she's free. I'd like to discuss her work in person. Is that all right with you?"

"As long as you find a restaurant with bulletproof glass," Aurora quipped. "I'm not sure I'm ready for a picnic in the park where we're too visible."

"I can arrange a private dining room at the Plains City Pub and Grill," he said. "Do you want to invite her or shall I?"

"I will. What time?"

He checked his watch. "We have to be at the hospice to meet Joy and my grandmother at two, so as soon as possible if she can get away. We have officers posted around the courthouse and the DA's office. They can escort her."

That brought a light chuckle. "You'll find that my cousin is a lot like me when it comes to being independent. She probably won't take kindly to being coddled."

Daniel felt his muscles tensing and stood tall. "There's a big difference between coddling and preventing a murder. Never forget why we're taking these precautions, Aurora."

The openness of her gaze when she looked into his eyes

touched his heart in unexpected ways. This woman fully trusted him despite their differences of opinion. It was as gratifying as if she'd just presented him with a gold medal for outstanding police work.

Without thinking, he raised one hand to cup her elbow, realizing that he'd been right when he'd suspected that she was trembling.

Somewhere down the hallway, a door slammed with a bang. Daniel startled and ducked slightly.

Aurora jumped and threw herself at him. He caught and held her. "It's okay. You're okay. That wasn't a shot."

Feeling her relax against his chest. he started to loosen his grip. She didn't let go. "I—I thought…"

"I know. Your nerves are wound a little tight."

"Yeah, you could say that." As she finally eased away, she again lifted her face to look at his.

Her breath was warm, minty. Time stopped. He saw her lips part slightly as if inviting a kiss. Did she have any idea what her actions were doing to his emotional reserve? Judging by the innocence of her expression, she might not.

He made no conscious decision to kiss her. It simply happened. The touch of their lips was brief and tender without the overly amorous reaction he'd experienced when other women threw themselves at him. Although it was a refreshing change, it reminded him how much older he was than the woman in his arms and how important it was to protect her, even from himself.

Gently grasping her shoulders, he set her away from him, wondering for a split second if she was angry. One look at her flushed cheeks and wide eyes told him she was anything but upset.

Her palms remained on his chest. She gasped. "Wow."

What could he say? That he was a fool? That was true but

far from helpful. At that point, he figured that anything he said could be misconstrued so he kept silent.

"I'm going to kennel Dakota before we leave for lunch. Make yourself at home here. I'll be back in a few."

His last glimpse of her as he left his office with his K-9 and closed the door behind them showed pure astonishment. Daniel huffed. If she thought *she* was surprised, she should spend a couple of minutes inside his brain and see what real shock was. That kiss almost defied description. It had been nothing like he'd expected, nothing that had reminded him of anyone else. Ever. And that was the biggest jolt of all. He was almost thirty-five. He'd kissed and been kissed more times than he could recall and never—never—had any woman's affections touched his heart the way Aurora's had.

That was wonderful. No...not wonderful. Terrible and frightening, assuming he intended to stick to his sensible plans for the rest of his life. Hadn't he learned enough by cleaning up after his father? By trying to salvage the lives that man had ruined? Marriage was not for him, period.

If he intended to protect Aurora, and he did, he'd better start by keeping a tight rein on his own emotions.

Maddie was obviously busy when Aurora was put through to her but she agreed to meet for lunch anyway.

"Agent Slater says he wants to talk to you about the case files you sent over."

"Anything to get out of the office for a break," Maddie said. "Everybody's uptight about the Carlson trial."

"Your evidence is solid?"

"Yes, but any time human opinion is involved, there's always a chance of losing. I'm just glad I'm not presenting opening arguments."

"You'll do fine," Aurora assured her. "We Martin women are strong and tough."

"But not bulletproof," Maddie said. "I can't believe you were standing right there when my car got shot full of holes, not to mention the prowler in my apartment."

"I wasn't exactly standing by your car," Aurora said with a smile. "I was kind of hunkered down on the ground with Daniel Slater and that pony-size Dane of his."

"My, my. Tell me more."

As Aurora said, "There's nothing to tell," she remembered the brief amazing kiss and wondered when that man, when *any* man, had managed to make her feel so special and vulnerable at the same time.

"Other than the fact he probably saved your life," Maddie countered.

"Yeah, well, there is that." She laughed to herself and at herself.

"And he is passable-looking if you don't mind old guys."

"What do you mean old? Daniel is perfect. He's mature and settled and smart and capable and, and…"

"Uh-huh. That's what I thought. So, does he know you're a card-carrying member of his fan club?"

"I sure hope not." Feeling warmth rising in her cheeks, Aurora was glad she was alone in his office. "The last thing he needs right now is some flighty woman chasing him."

"You're not flighty," Maddie said. Aurora could tell her cousin was laughing.

"I have felt kind of disconnected since Mom died," she admitted. "My dad's no help. I'm sorry if I've pushed you away lately. Grief does funny things to people."

Maddie sobered. "I know what you mean. You're still the sister I never had. So keep your head down and concentrate on surviving whatever's going on, will you?"

"You too."

"Always.

"So, we're on for lunch?" Aurora asked.

"Let's make it eleven thirty."

"Okay. Earlier is better. We're going to see Joy's mother in hospice at two," Aurora told her. "I've never met Serena but Daniel wants me to go along this time."

"Really? Wow. That sounds like he has a thing for you."

"Not really. I think it's mostly because he wants to keep an eye on me and is afraid I'll wander off on my own."

"Is that likely?" the ADA asked, sounding concerned.

"No, ma'am. It's been a long time since anybody volunteered to look after my best interests and I'm managing to tolerate Daniel's micromanagement. Besides, Joy is the sweetest little thing and I want to support her in case the visit doesn't go well."

"Serena's that bad off?"

"Yes," Aurora said soberly.

"Then wait until you see me," Maddie said brightly. "I got a new cut to make me look tougher for the trial. My hair stands up in the cutest spikes."

Aurora almost laughed in spite of their serious conversation. How like Maddie it was to change the subject in order to cheer her up. She and her cousin had often mimicked each other in the past but matching her hair to Maddie's this time was definitely not happening.

"Whatever makes you happy, cuz, but I'm sticking with long hair I can put up if I want to. See you soon."

She had just ended the call when Daniel returned, his spine rigid, his demeanor officious. In spite of the off-putting attitude, Aurora smiled at him. "We're on for lunch. Maddie will meet us in front of the courthouse at eleven thirty."

He glanced at his watch. "No problem. I have a few team members to check in with and I'll be done here."

"Any news about the gun trafficking?" she asked. Seeing him raise an eyebrow at her, she added, "It's not like I'm a civilian messing in police business, you know."

It looked as if he was upset about something and that concerned her. If he was sorry he'd kissed her, she intended to remind him that it took both of them to decide to do it. Asking him however was out of the question. She squared her shoulders to mimic his formality.

"There have been sightings of some of the traffickers in Fargo, which isn't all that surprising. The ones we have in custody have legal representation so the questioning is slow. The best we've been able to do is get bail denied."

"Is Brandon Murray footing the bill for the lawyers?"

"Yes, and no," Daniel said with a frown. "He's the primary contact but as far as we can tell, he's not the money man."

"Really?" Thoughts of a personal nature fled as she tried to figure out who could be supporting their primary suspect. "Is that part of why you haven't been able to track him down? He has influential friends? What about his family? I mean besides Hal."

"I think that's part of what's made him so volatile. He's an orphan. His brother was all he had."

"I wish forensics had been more help. Maybe if we had more clues…"

The look he gave her was unreadable. "Please," Daniel said flatly. "No more clues that involve people getting shot at."

She was quick on the defense. "I didn't mean that." Which was true, sort of. The trouble was, the fewer encounters the police had with the gun trafficking group, the less likely they were to track them down. And they were still left wondering whose gun the bullet holes in Maddie's car had come from. And why.

"Being a target is *not* my favorite pastime," she told him. "Coming up with leads that put criminals in jail is different. I'll take my clues however I can get them."

As she watched, Daniel took his gun out of a shoulder

holster, checked the ammo, then replaced it with a snap before straightening his jacket. "All right. Let's get this show on the road."

NINE

By the time Daniel and Aurora reached the courthouse, he had received a dispatch for that very place. Someone had phoned in a bomb threat and the warning was being taken seriously. The formidable stone building was surrounded by police cars, lights flashing, and a cordon of officers was setting up a temporary barricade.

To his surprise, Maddie Martin was already outside, briefcase in hand, purse strap slung over one shoulder of her suit coat. Daniel did a double take. Whoever had said she looked exactly like Aurora had been right—and wrong. He unlocked the door and stepped out, engine running.

"Slide in behind the wheel for now while I get my team assigned to specific areas," he said. "Lunch may be a little delayed."

"The story of my life," Maddie said with a brief smile. "What a morning."

He watched as the two women embraced like long-lost sisters and was reminded of all the family time he'd missed by not meeting Serena as a child. He was also struck by how much alike the cousins faces and physiques were. If not for Maddie's wild spikey hairdo, it was easy to see how they could be mistaken for each other, particularly when Aurora was driving the car registered to her look-alike.

Daniel radioed Kenyon Graves first. He and Peanut, the gun

and explosives-detecting beagle, were already inside, leading the DGTF portion of the search for a hidden bomb.

"Graves."

"Kenyon, it's me, Daniel. How are you doing? Managing okay?"

"If you're asking if my past has surfaced to make me unstable, the answer is no. Peanut is doing fine too. If there's a bomb in any of the rooms we search, he'll find it."

"Good. What's your projected time frame?"

"I know Lucy and Piper are checking the basement. If we had a dozen Peanuts and Pipers on the team, we'd be done in an hour. Regular officers are searching the courtrooms. West, Lucy and I will move our dogs to the judges' chambers when we finish here." Daniel was grateful to have Kenyon on the team, along with Lucy Lopez and her bomb-detection K-9 and West Cole, whose K-9, Gus, specialized in weapons detection. While Dakota was skilled in weapons detection and could help them, she was also trained in protection—and right now protecting Maddie and Aurora was his top priority.

"What about the DA's offices?"

"West and Jenna are checking those. So far, so good. They're clear." The two officers and their K-9s would have that part of the search well in hand.

"Okay. Thanks. I'll be off duty this afternoon for an hour or so to visit my sister. If you turn up anything, call my personal number."

"Copy that."

Daniel paused to scan the street and other surroundings. Bright sunlight had burned off the early morning fog. A few stubborn patches of snow lingered in shaded areas but, by and large, the November day was surprisingly warm.

He checked in with the local incident commander and touched base with a fire engine on standby before returning to his vehicle and opening the driver's door. "If you ladies still want lunch I suggest we grab something quick and eat in the car. It's not wise being exposed like this."

"Do you think the bomb threat was made to get us out into the open?" Maddie asked. "It did occur to me."

"Possibly." He was eyeing the rear compartment where Dakota usually rode. "I'm a little short on comfortable seats. We'll have to make do."

"Maddie and I can scooch in here together," Aurora said, glancing behind her. "You can't ask Maddie to ride where the dog does."

That brought a wry smile. "Actually, I was thinking of asking you to sit back there. You're dressed for it and she isn't."

Aurora laughed good-naturedly before settling in the back.

It did occur to him he could've borrowed one of the patrol cars but since he didn't plan on going far and his SUV was armored, it was the safest place for all of them, at least temporarily. He'd never had reason to transport more than one other person and their working dog so the vehicle was usually ideal.

"Okay," he said, glancing at Maddie. "There's a good chance this bomb scare was a ruse to get you out of the courthouse where you'd make a better target. Let's get you both out of here. We still need to eat so we should go to lunch."

"Good. I'm starving," the ADA said with a smile. "If you're buying, even better."

A glance in the rearview showed him Aurora's blush as Maddie laughed lightly. The women might resemble each other in many ways but it was clear that one was much bolder. Backing out and pulling into traffic, he decided to use the drive time to settle a few things. "I've been in touch with Lorelei Danvers about moving each of you to new homes for the time being," he said, continuing before either of his companions had a chance to protest. "It's not going to be easy to keep you close to your jobs without giving away your locations so we'll take it one day at a time. She'll have Maddie picked up at the courthouse, assuming it checks out by quitting time. If not, they can make other arrangements. I'll be keeping you, Aurora, with me this afternoon until we see if it's feasible for you to be relocated. If we do move you, it has to be done covertly. There's no sense changing locations if we do it publicly." He paused. "Agreed?"

"As long as I can still work," Maddie said.

Aurora agreed. "Same here. I can't think of a safer place to work than inside a police station, can you?"

"Did you get a chance to confirm the whereabouts of the felons I listed?" Maddie asked him.

"Yes. Kyra Fellowes's alibi for the time of the drive-by shooting is solid and her former boyfriend is in jail in California. How about others? You said there was a list."

"How much time have you got?" Maddie said wryly.

By the time lunch was finished, the courthouse had been declared safe and Daniel had delivered Maddie back to her office. Aurora would have preferred to have spent more quality time with her cousin but little Joy needed moral support and she was actually looking forward to helping the sweet toddler. Jack and Beau delivered the others to the hospice lobby where they all met. Listening to the men's conversation was unsettling.

"Sorry, Daniel," Jack said. "I know it's not what you want to hear but I really don't think your house is totally safe unless some of us are staying there 24/7."

"You know I can't justify that," Daniel said. "I pushed the rules hard in order to station you there this morning."

"Then I suggest you reconsider a safe house for your family too, since last night's prowler seems to be so well connected."

"The fancy lawyer, you mean?"

"Yes. He's invoking client privilege and won't disclose who

hired him to represent the guy so it can't be an innocent third party."

"I think you're right," Daniel said. "And our stubborn CSI has finally agreed to move if we can find a convenient place."

Daniel offered his hand and Jack shook it. "Thanks for your help looking after my family."

"Anytime. Just holler. Beau has a doggie crush on Dakota." He looked around. "Where is she, anyway?"

"I left her back at the station since we were coming here after lunch. She needs the R & R and it wouldn't be good to bring her into such a sterile environment, even if it is legal."

"Sensible, as always," Jack said with a smile. "Okay. I'll hit the road. See you tomorrow?"

"I'm sure. There's a high-profile murder trial starting at the courthouse. A few of us will need to do another explosives sweep before then. I'll probably put Lucy, West and Kenyon on it again. I definitely want Lucy and Piper and Kenyon and Peanut."

"Copy that." Jack gave a casual salute that looked more like parting gesture than a military one.

Turning, Daniel rejoined them and they all entered the deathly silent, sterile-smelling environment. Joy reached for him and Aurora was pleased to see him scoop her up and balance her on one hip. She followed the family as they quietly entered Serena's room and stood around the bed. There was a palpable sense of peace in the room. A nurse in blue scrubs stood to one side and nodded a greeting.

"Hey, sis," Daniel said, sounding more upbeat than Aurora knew he felt. "You have company."

There was a gleam in the young woman's green eyes when she opened them and smiled at her daughter. "Hi, honey."

Joy clung tightly to Daniel's neck and hid her face against his shoulder. He tried to turn her. She resisted.

Catherine handed Serena a fresh tissue and bent to kiss her

on the forehead. "I see you're wearing the scarf I gave you. I thought real silk would be easier on your skin than cotton or synthetics"

Serena's thin fingers ruffled the loose ends. "It's beautiful. I love it. Later, when I don't need it anymore, maybe you can give it to Joy to remember me by after I'm gone."

Joy looked over Daniel's shoulder at Aurora, then shifted to gaze down at the bed. "Mama's goin' to Heaven, huh?"

"Yes," Aurora said softly. She smiled at the child, then at Serena. "Do you belong to Jesus?"

Tears began to trail down Serena's cheeks. "Oh, yes. And thank you for asking. I didn't know how to explain my faith to Joy. I'm not afraid of death. The only sad part is that I'll have to be away from my baby."

Approaching, Aurora spoke to Joy. "Would you like me to help you give your mama a hug? We'll be very careful so we don't hurt her."

"Uh-huh."

And just like that, the previously reluctant toddler let go of Daniel and reached for Aurora, who then lowered her gently onto the bed into Serena's waiting arms.

The hospital atmosphere ceased to matter and their surroundings faded away as Aurora's hands came to rest gently on the pair, one on Joy's fine curls and one caressing Serena's tear dampened cheek as if giving a benediction.

When Serena began to whisper a prayer, Aurora joined her. Their eyes met. Understanding flowed, as did mutual tears. "Take care of my baby."

What could she say? How could she make a vow like that? And yet, it seemed to be the right thing to do.

"I promise to always be there for her if she needs me," Aurora whispered, hoping that Daniel wouldn't take it wrong. She didn't mean to usurp his authority or invade his family; she simply wanted to give a dying woman some hope.

A sidelong glance was all it took to assure Aurora that she had not overstepped. The stalwart federal agent was blinking back tears of his own and almost smiling at her.

For the time she was with Daniel's family, Aurora had felt at peace, even when she was consoling Serena and Joy. The bond between mother and daughter was one that she understood, particularly since the loss of her own mom. That was how life was, she told herself. Loved ones came and went in spite of anyone's intervention and all you were left with was fond memories. And faith, she added immediately. Without her faith to lean on, she knew she would have been far more devastated. Yet that didn't keep a loss from hurting, it simply provided reassurance of a reunion someday. To ask, to yearn for more was not only futile, it was self-defeating.

Leaning back in the passenger seat of Daniel's SUV as he drove them back to the station, she closed her eyes and gave herself over to the prodding of her conscience. Was that her problem? Was she fighting the reality that her mother was gone because she so wanted it to be otherwise? That possibility had never occurred to her before. Now, she gave it a place in her mind, if not her heart.

Daniel broke into her reverie. "Lorelei Danvers, the US marshal on my team, has arranged to move Nana and Joy tonight."

Aurora's head snapped around and she blinked to clear her thoughts. "Catherine agreed?"

"We're doing what we think is best for Joy."

"I get that. I do. But why leave that house? It's a fortress." It was clear by his expression, even though his face was in profile as he drove, that he'd been asking himself the same questions. His explanation however made sense.

"My team is close to shutting down the gun traffickers. It's only a matter of time. We've confiscated multiple shipments and are finding caches in several nearby national parks. That's federal land. When they chose to bury and hide their illegal merchandise on government property, they were overconfident. It was a big mistake. One they'll pay for soon." He took a deep breath before continuing. "We've always known the target the other night at my place could've been me. One of Jack's confidential informants worked for Brandon and Hal Jones/Murray. He's positive that the death of Hal unhinged Brandon. Killing his girlfriend disgusted the confidential informant enough to make him talk."

"I heard that on the video call." Aurora wanted to roll her hands, one over the other, as if tumbling downhill, to hurry him up. Instead, she clasped her fingers together in her lap and waited.

"There is a shipment of guns due to be moved soon, probably this week, destined for the Badlands. We're setting up to intercept and hopefully capture what's left of the gang." His hesitancy bothered her. She swiveled as far as the seat belt would allow to face him. To see what was so troubling. "And…what else?"

"If I needed proof of who the shooter on my property was working for, I got it when he was arrested inside the fence. We haven't gotten a confession but he's definitely part of the trafficking operation. We have telephoto pictures of him with some of the others."

Her mind raced. How could that be? "But, if that's true, then why did he shoot at Maddie's car?"

"It may not have been him," Daniel said. He was slowly shaking his head. "I know you thought it was the same man you saw drive by but it might not have been."

"He looked like the picture you showed me."

"I know. But the car was speeding and you were moving at the time, so it's possible you made a mistake."

She pulled a face and folded her arms. "Okay. Go on. What else?"

"My team suspects that I was the target, not you."

"Is that supposed to make me relax? Because if it is, it's not working."

He huffed. "No. It's supposed to explain why I need to move my family. The local PD has assigned a couple of officers to get your cousin to and from the courthouse for the trial that starts tomorrow."

"Maybe you don't need to protect me at all," Aurora offered. "If the first shooter was after you, maybe she and I are both safe now."

He shook his head. "That doesn't explain the guys in her apartment."

"Hmm. I'd forgotten about them." She brightened. "Still, not my problem, right?"

"Except for your ability to identify the drive-by gunman."

"You just told me I got that *wrong*!"

"I know that and you know that but that's no guarantee *they* know it."

She rolled her eyes. "You're a very exasperating person."

Daniel chuckled. "So I've been told."

"Okay. Let me get this straight. There's a criminal out to get me, a criminal out to get you, a crazed gunman after my cousin and a big gun bust about to take place. Anything else?"

"Yes. My team members and their families are all in the crosshairs of the Jones/Murray gang. That's not supposition, it's fact. We have info from more than one source that confirms the threats. You, by association at the murder scene of Lila Pierce, have been added to the list. I don't like it any more than you do, but that's how it is."

Slumping back against the seat, Aurora sighed. What he'd said made a little sense but only assuming he was right. "I'm still not convinced that I should be included," she argued. "If the prowler at your house was after you and we assume the shooter who damaged Maddie's car was too, I should be in the clear."

"That's a lot of assumption."

"It's more likely than what you came up with."

"You're a hardheaded woman," Daniel said, "Know that?"

Trying not to smile, she made another silly face at him. "What took you so long?"

"Oh, I knew it before. I'm just a touch amazed to see how unconcerned you seem to be about being shot at."

"Well, I don't have a death wish, if that's what you're hinting at. I fully intend to live as long as possible."

"That's comforting to hear."

"What I'm trying to say is that I think you're overreacting. All I have to do is go home and mind my own business and I'll be fine."

"You hope."

"Tell you what," she said, choosing her words carefully, "Run me by my place and at least let me get some more clothes. The stuff Jenna picked isn't exactly what I like to wear."

"We can buy you new stuff."

"I need to go feed my goldfish," Aurora said with a lopsided smile.

Daniel's head snapped around. He was scowling. "You have a goldfish?"

She had to laugh. "No, but I might buy one soon. Come on, Agent Slater, be a pal. Take me to my apartment. Please?"

Watching varied emotions crossing his face, she could tell when he'd made his decision.

"Fine. But we go pick up Dakota first. I feel like I'm only half prepared when she's not by my side."

"Works for me. I kind of miss the sweetheart, myself."

"She's not a pet," Daniel warned.

Aurora chuckled again. "I've seen her relate to Joy. She

may be formidable when she's wearing her K-9 unit vest but take it off and she's a big hairy teddy bear."

"With a tail wag that can knock Joy down if Dakota's not careful. Get thumped by it and you may get a bruise."

"I'll take my chances," Aurora said.

When Daniel replied, "That's what I'm afraid of," she knew he was no longer referring to his canine partner. The concept almost made her grin until she realized he may have meant he feared she'd be hurt physically in some other way. While her personal thoughts had been focused on their budding relationship, Daniel was obviously thinking of the deadly aspects surrounding them all and she figured it would be best if she too remembered just how much danger still lurked. Complacency could be as lethal as actual bullets.

TEN

There had been no surveillance ordered for Aurora's apartment building because she was no longer supposed to be in residence, so Daniel approached cautiously with Dakota at his side. He'd picked the K-9 up earlier and told Aurora to wait in his bullet-proof car when he'd parked in front of her building. She did not.

"You're determined to give me gray hair, aren't you?" he said over his shoulder.

"A little gray will make you look distinguished."

"Says you."

He stood aside as she keyed in the code to unlock the exterior door, then resumed the lead when she opened it. Dakota seemed as relaxed as she ever got while working so he wasn't too concerned. Wary, yes, but not worried.

"I'm on the ground floor. Straight ahead," Aurora said. "Second door on the right."

"Got it." He paused in front of her apartment. "All right. No more fun and games, lady. Dakota and I will make a sweep before you enter. Understand?" When she nodded, he held out one hand. "Key?"

Seeing her open her mouth as if to speak, then close it again, Daniel was satisfied she'd forced herself to hold in one of her snappy comebacks. He didn't take everything seriously in life and could appreciate good banter. He simply knew where to draw the line to preserve a sense of duty and responsibility. For the present, no one else was as responsible for Aurora Martin as he was.

Letting Dakota take the lead, he unlocked and entered the silent apartment while Aurora waited just outside the doorway. The blinds were open to admit enough daylight to navigate. The K-9's nose was to the ground, then checking the furniture as they walked past. Because his concentration was on the dog and the task at hand, it took him an extra moment to realize Aurora was calling his name from the hallway.

"Daniel? Daniel?"

Rather than answer and reveal his position before Dakota had completed her search, he simply paused to listen.

Her voice rose to almost a screech. "Daniel!"

When she'd first seen the man in the parka approaching from the opposite end of the hall, Aurora hadn't sensed anything odd. When he'd raised his head to look at her and she saw his ski mask however, everything changed.

A gloved hand reached toward her. She lunged toward the doorway and screamed, "Daniel!"

The stranger grabbed her coat. She twisted and fought. Tried to turn enough to hit or kick him. Her boots slipped on the slick tile and she would have crashed to the floor if her attacker had not been holding onto her.

Grasping one flailing arm at the wrist, he began to drag her down the hallway, away from her apartment. Her boots slid as she fought for a footing, writhing against his much larger body and trying to wrench free. Making a fist with her free hand she swung wildly, trying for his face and coming up short. "Help! Daniel!"

Everything was happening so fast that Aurora was disoriented. The assailant slapped her so hard her vision blurred.

She began to sag, realized the extra weight was causing him trouble and let herself go limp.

He flipped her over so he could grasp both arms. Someone was shouting. A tan blur loomed. *Dakota!* Knocked to the floor and breathless, she curled into the fetal position and covered her head.

Panic kept Aurora from realizing right away that the strong hands gripping her upper arms now belonged to friend, not foe. Then she recognized a human face. Daniel's face. He looked angry and relieved at the same time. Dakota had passed them by and stood barking at the exit door.

Daniel held her firm, forcing her to focus. "Are you hurt?"

"No…"

He abruptly set her aside and ran to join his K-9. Aurora saw him open the door, look both ways, then turn back to her.

"Go get him!" Aurora shouted.

"No. He might not have been alone. I can't leave you."

Folding her arms and hugging herself, she tried to control the tremors shooting through her. "What would he want with me? I mean, he was trying to drag me away."

Although she saw concern and compassion in his expression he nevertheless said, "I told you coming here was a bad idea."

"Yeah, well, we're here now." She looked toward her once-welcoming apartment and shivered. "If you're not going to go after the guy, you may as well come with me while I pack a bag."

"Well, I'm not about to go chasing a phantom. You didn't happen to pull off his glove or mask so Dakota can get a clear scent, did you?"

"No. I was trying to get away from him, not collect souvenirs." To her chagrin she sounded decidedly unfriendly so she added, "Look, I'm sorry I lost my temper. I know you're doing your best. Just remember, so am I."

She didn't expect him to agree with her. They had spent hours and hours together lately but really didn't know each other on a personal basis. Daniel couldn't help it if their forced nearness had sent her emotions into orbit. Perhaps she was naturally quicker to form bonds than he was. Given his up-bringing, that was likely. And, truth be told, she was giving him the best she had to offer, even if it wasn't coming from professional police training. She didn't have a gun, nor did she want one, but she did have her wits and the courage to fight when the situation called for action.

Daniel drew Dakota to his side and man and dog stepped back together. "Go," he said. "Get your stuff and let's get out of here. The longer we stay the greater the chance that your mystery attacker will come back with reinforcements."

"He was very real," she insisted.

"Oh, I know he was," Daniel replied. "I haven't seen you that pale since we were shot at next to Maddie's car."

"I have to look the part to convince you?" Merely asking the question shook her confidence in their tenuous relationship.

"No. I believed you the second I heard you screaming my name. Nobody would sound that scared unless the threat was very real. It's my fault. I should have kept you with me while I searched your apartment."

He was shaking his head slowly and gazing into her eyes with such self-deprecation she instantly wanted to comfort him. "It's not anybody's fault," Aurora said, placing her hand lightly on his upper arm without stopping to think first.

Daniel glanced down at her touch, then silently placed Dakota in a sit and opened his arms.

Nobody had to tell Aurora he was offering the same solace she'd been yearning to give him. The merest hesitation might change everything, might cause him to reconsider, and that was the last thing she wanted.

In two small steps, she was in his arms, her cheek pressed

to his chest, listening to the rapid beating of his heart. Her arms slid around his waist and she felt the top of his gun and its holster. That was enough to remind her how serious their current situation was and how unwise it was to delay. Smiling up at him, she eased off.

"I'll pack a few things and be back in a flash," she took a step. "Don't go away."

Daniel returned her smile even though the good humor failed to reach his green eyes. When he said, "Never," Aurora couldn't help wishing he was right.

True to her word, Aurora didn't keep him waiting long. He used the time to report the attempted abduction and advise his team. Nothing else had happened since the bomb scare at the courthouse and Lorelai Danvers had secured a safe temporary dwelling for his grandmother and Joy. They had also placed a guard on Serena's hospital room just in case the Jones/Murray gang decided to widen their list of targets. Police officers did a good job protecting each other and the citizens they served but unfortunately, while they were off doing that, their families were vulnerable.

He left Dakota to guard Aurora for the few minutes it took him to inspect his SUV for tampering. When he was certain all was well, he escorted them to the car. While he was loading the dog and wiping icy slush off her paws, Aurora let herself in the passenger door and fastened her seat belt. By the time he slid behind the wheel, she was ready to go.

"I see you got some warm gloves. Smart," he said, making casual conversation in the hope she wouldn't ask anything personal. First, he had no idea why he had embraced her again. And second, he wondered if she'd assumed too much about his feelings. If he had been alone with his K-9, he might have talked it out with Dakota just to sort out his jumbled thoughts.

Since he was not, he figured the smartest thing he could do was avoid the subject.

"Thanks." She was again rubbing her hands together in front of the heater vent, gloves or no gloves. "Winter tends to sneak up on me sometimes."

"November is never that warm."

"Right."

Daniel knew she was studying his profile as he drove and probably itching to talk about something other than the South Dakota weather, so he provided another safe topic. "My team and I may have to leave Plains City to set up a sting for the traffickers soon."

"How soon?"

"Don't worry. We'll—I'll—make sure you aren't left without protection. The local PD is very capable."

"I know. I've worked with them for years."

"Not that many years. You're practically a kid."

"And you're Methuselah. I know. You told me. So, where am I staying tonight? With Catherine or Maddie?"

"Neither. Catherine and Joy are somewhere away from town so they won't be spotted easily. If I took you there, we'd be leaving a trail for the gang to follow."

"Maddie too?"

"No. She's staying put with extra guards. The Derek Carlson trial is a big deal and she's needed in court."

"For how long?"

"As long as it takes. Murder trials aren't quick. They shouldn't be. Justice needs to be served cautiously and thoroughly."

Aurora sighed. "I get it. I just wish we could sort out all the vindictive criminals instead of lumping their actions together."

"We can. We will," Daniel promised. "One day, one problem at a time. I've had Cheyenne Chen working on the list your cousin gave us. Something will break soon. I know it will.

"As long as it's not one of us that *breaks*," Aurora gibed. She paused. "It must be very hard."

His head snapped around and he frowned. "What?"

"Being responsible for a whole team of law enforcement professionals and all their K-9 partners while you try to catch criminals."

Sighing, he nodded. "It is." Although he could have said more, wanted to unburden himself to her, he held back. As long as she was taking the multiple threats seriously and following his orders, he saw no reason to frighten her more. Reality was bad enough without imagining all the possible scenarios that criminals might create in their attempts to thwart him and his K-9 team. He'd almost lost Jack Donadio once and had thought Kenyon Graves was gone for good until recently.

Keeping them and the rest of his team safe until their assignment was complete was the most important assignment of his career, perhaps of his entire life. He didn't intend to fail. That was not an option.

ELEVEN

The last place Aurora expected Daniel to take her was back to his fortified home. Yes, she felt safe there but in view of his opinion about the house being identified, it seemed illogical.

She peered out at the property as the wrought iron gate swung open. "Color me confused. I thought you weren't in favor of any of us staying here."

"I wasn't. I'm still not. But unfortunately Plains City is woefully short on available safe houses."

"That's what I was trying to tell you in the first place."

"I know, I know. Plains City has two, both occupied."

"Nothing else is available?"

"No. Joy and Nana have been taken to the one on a cul-de-sac not too far from the police station. There was a vegetation fire—an arson—near it a few months back but the trees and shrubs are recovering. The windows are bullet-resistant and the exterior walls reinforced, just in case."

"Isn't that just like your house?"

"Pretty much, yes," Daniel said.

Lost in thought, she let herself drift away from the present and was only slightly aware that Daniel had pulled his SUV around to the rear of the house and was preparing to enter the underground garage again.

The door slowly rose. The car began to inch forward. Suddenly, Dakota began to bark as if she'd just spotted something deadly.

Daniel slammed the SUV into Reverse and floored the accelerator. Tires squealed on asphalt. The vehicle fishtailed and straightened facing the opposite direction.

Shouting, "Down!" he gave Aurora's shoulder a push. In the rear, Dakota continued to sound off.

Even if she'd been paying closer attention, which she had not, Aurora doubted she'd know what was going on.

Something pinged against a side window, shattering the glass into spidery cracks that nevertheless stayed in place, although she assumed further shots might penetrate it in spite of its defensive characteristics.

She stayed low, watching sideways as Daniel reported, "Shots fired," and drew his weapon.

Stunned that he was actually getting out to personally face their attackers, she made a grab for him and missed. "Don't."

He ignored her. Crouching behind the open SUV door, he took aim, paused, then slammed it shut with her inside.

Never had she felt so helpless. So useless. A remote command raised the hatchback for Dakota's exit, then closed it again. In moments, both the officer and his K-9 were gone.

They had left her. Just like that. And not only was she unarmed, she was as exposed to the threat as they were.

The urge to flee was almost strong enough to make Aurora bolt from the car. Almost but not quite. Her survival instinct overrode all others and she hunkered down to wait. There was a chance that whoever had shot at them didn't know she was with Daniel so showing herself would be foolish. There was an even greater chance that he and Dakota would locate and overpower their assailant or assailants quickly.

That was her most fervent prayer, right after, *Father, take care of all of us.*

* * *

Dakota led the way past the side of the house. That was enough to assure Daniel the shooter was outside, not in the garage, which was comforting. At least his home defenses hadn't been breached. Plus, the cameras should show enough recorded data to tell him how and when the property had been accessed.

Gun at the ready, he pressed his back against an outer wall and prepared to release Dakota. First, he shouted, "Police. Come out with your hands up or I'll send the dog."

No one responded.

At Daniel's side, his K-9 was fidgeting. She was technically seated, as he'd commanded, but her hindquarters quivered and her front paws danced in place.

"Last chance," Daniel called. "Give yourself up." He began to count aloud. "One. Two. Three. Four," and on *five* he unsnapped Dakota's leash.

The K-9 was off like a shot with Daniel following. Her trajectory drew his attention to a hedge near the iron gate. Shadows. At least two.

"Stop or I'll shoot," Daniel shouted at them.

They didn't and he didn't. Dropping fleeing suspects was against policy for good reason. He might have been in danger once but their running away changed everything—until one of the figures stopped, turned and fired.

The bright red muzzle flash told Daniel exactly where the antagonist was and he returned fire. Once. Successfully.

The shooter screamed and dropped as his partner scaled the gate. Dakota closed in and clamped her jaw around the first man's wrist to keep him from shooting again. She held him in spite of his screeching and squirming until Daniel caught up, disarmed him and gave the command to release.

The other assailant had disappeared into the dim evening light but Daniel had stopped one of them. He radioed in the location and circumstances to update his original report, leashed his K-9 and administered first aid while he waited for backup and an ambulance and thanked God Aurora was safe in his fortified car.

Aurora had not intended to sound miffed when Daniel finally returned to her but she'd had plenty of time to work up a snit and some of it spilled out.

"You *left* me!"

"Dakota and I caught the bad guy."

"Wonderful." Straightening as she left the SUV, she dusted herself off as if she'd been crouched in dirt. "Suppose there'd been more than one?"

"Actually, there were two. But they stuck together so it all worked out."

"Terrific. It never occurred to you that there might be more than that?"

"It did. I made a judgment call. You were far safer locked in the car."

"I suppose I should be thankful you were right." She pulled a face.

It didn't help her mood when he started to smile and said, "You're welcome."

"I didn't mean it as a compliment."

"You're still welcome." He gestured at the house. "Let's go inside and let these officers do their jobs."

Still trembling in spite of knowing the danger had passed, Aurora glanced at the damaged car. "The slug has to be inside."

"Why?" He'd moved closer to her so she began to edge toward the rear door.

"Because it didn't exit on this side."

"Logical." Daniel started toward the area where they'd first been accosted. "Unless it's out here, on the ground."

"Is that possible?" She strongly doubted that any safety glass would repel the actual projectile.

"Not likely, no," he answered. "They'll probably need a magnet to find it if it was flattened or fractured on impact."

Aurora folded her arms to draw the front of her coat closer to her body. "Then let's let them do the looking. I'm starting to get chilled again."

"Some of that shaking is probably from the surge of adrenaline you got when we arrived. Come on inside. I'll fix you something to warm you up. Catherine usually leaves a pot of coffee waiting when she knows I'll be home soon."

"She's gone, remember? You're going to have to take care of yourself for a change."

"You don't cook?"

"Ha! Not if I can help it," Aurora said. "If you want toast, I can probably handle it. Anything more is iffy. As long as I can afford takeout or DoorDash, I don't starve and my kitchen stays clean all the time. Win-win."

Chuckling, he led the way with Dakota at his side. "There's a certain perverse logic to your rationale."

"Thanks, I think."

He held the lower level door for her, then paused to remove Dakota's official gear before tending to his own needs.

While she waited, Aurora took in the command center monitors again. "You know," she said, "this is the perfect place to sleep. We can watch your whole place."

"I was planning for us to sleep down here anyway," Daniel said. "I'd rather we stayed together under the circumstances."

"Works for me." Aurora smiled and pointed at an overstuffed, comfy-looking recliner. "Dibs on that."

Daniel began to chuckle. "Can't, it's taken."

"You can crash on the sofa instead."

"Nope. Sorry," he said, still clearly amused. "Dakota

claimed that chair the first time I brought her home. She doesn't like to share."

"You're going to let a *dog* have first choice?" Aurora wasn't nearly as surprised as she was pretending to be. She fisted both hands on her hips and rolled her eyes at him to add humor. There was something appealing about silly repartee coming on the heels of a life-threatening experience and she wanted to continue to enjoy it.

She could tell Daniel was fighting the urge to laugh more because his lips were twitching and those greenish eyes of his glinted with suppressed mirth as he said, "Special Officer Dakota Slater is my partner, on and off the job. She will always get preference over anyone else."

"Then she's very fortunate," Aurora replied, also feigning self-control. "I suppose if one of us has to sleep on this floor, it's only right that it be one of us. I'm sure I'll find the couch comfortable."

"I'll run upstairs and check to make sure there are no problems while I grab some pillows and blankets."

She had taken off her coat and sat to remove her boots herself. "Okay. Shall I go try to find us something to eat?"

He paused in the doorway and leaned back in, smiling. "Sure. Bread's in the fridge and the toaster's on the counter by the coffeepot."

Chuckling softly to herself, Aurora was certain she heard her host actually laughing as he climbed the stairs to the main level. It was a welcome, heartwarming sound, almost enough to make her forget she was there, in his home, because someone kept trying to kill them.

TWELVE

To Daniel's surprise, Dakota deferred to Aurora about occupying the recliner. Instead of standing there staring at the interloper, the dog seemed to know that the woman needed her favorite sleeping spot and took up a place on the floor next to the sofa. As soon as Daniel had completed a final safety check, he stretched out on the couch, pulled up a light blanket and tucked a pillow under his head. All he had to do from that position was open his eyes and he could see Aurora. She'd pulled a quilt up to her chin and fallen asleep almost immediately, which relieved him enough to allow him to do the same.

Morning came with a start when Dakota barked. If her tone had been deep and menacing, Daniel would have reached for his gun. He opened his eyes and saw her prancing around and wagging her tail. "What? It can't be morning." But it was.

Across the room, Aurora stretched and yawned. "Um. I think it is. I'm starving."

"Do you know how to make coffee?"

"It's not that much harder than toast," she cracked back, smiling. "I think I can handle it."

"Okay." He threw off his blanket and reached for his boots. She too arose but stayed in her stocking feet. "Meet you in the kitchen."

He was picking up his gear and phone after donning a jacket. Dakota beat him to the exit and continued to fidget.

She was through the door and galloping over the lawn the instant he released her.

As he waited for his K-9 to be ready to go back inside, he strolled across the driveway to his SUV, taking in the damage and keeping his eyes open for clues. The CSIs last night must have done a good job, he concluded, because there were no signs of the bullet or shell casing.

Dakota was loping along the fence line, showing little interest, so Daniel relaxed. Curious, he phoned his office to see if the shooter had admitted anything.

Jack Donadio fielded his call. "Morning, Daniel. Sleep well?"

"Everything was peaceful, thankfully. Anything new on the perps?"

"Not that I know of. Your latest contribution to the Plains City jail has the same lawyer the first one does."

"That figures."

"Yeah, that's what I thought too."

"We're…" Jack stopped talking. In the background, Daniel could hear a radio dispatch. *All available units to the Courthouse.*

His first thought was for Maddie. "Talk to me, Jack. What's going on?"

"Shots fired at the courthouse," Jack replied.

"Details?"

"Not yet. Will you be responding?"

"Yes, as soon as I can get all my ducks in a row here. I can't run off and leave a witness."

"Got it. I'll see what else I can find out and get back to you ASAP."

Daniel was already heading for the house. He whistled for Dakota and she came at a run. They went through the door together and Daniel took the stairs two at a time.

He burst into the kitchen.

Startled, Aurora fumbled a coffee cup and almost dropped it. "What's wrong?"

"I'm not sure. What time does your cousin usually go to work?"

"It depends on the day and her schedule. Why?"

"Just put your boots on and grab your jacket. We're heading for town."

"Okay, okay. Why won't you tell me what's happened?"

"I'm not sure. All I know is there were shots fired at the courthouse. I don't have any other details."

Looking stunned, all Aurora said was, "Maddie," before she ran toward the lower level. Watching her go, Daniel hoped their instincts were both wrong but given the previous threats and the scheduled trial today, he was afraid they might actually be right. Maddie was going to be there and had been targeted before, or so they thought. If it had happened again and Aurora wasn't anywhere nearby, then their earlier conclusions stood.

His team and Aurora weren't the only ones with targets on their backs. The assistant DA had officially joined their group.

Aurora settled for loosely tying her shoelaces and grabbing her jacket. She cared less about being properly dressed than she did about getting to town and making sure her cousin was all right.

Seated in Daniel's SUV, she put up her hood and clasped her arms over her jacket to ward off the cold air whooshing through his partially broken side window. It was making a whistling, moaning sound that lent a foreboding soundtrack to their mission. "Did they say if anyone was hit?" she asked.

Daniel shook his head. "No. Jack just got the dispatch. I told him we were responding from home."

Home? The word stuck in her mind. What was home anyway, other than a place to sleep and eat? It had meant more to her as a child of course, but events of late had tarnished those sweet memories and left her feeling as if she had no real home. There was her apartment, which had been violated, as had Maddie's. And there was the home she'd once shared with her parents, now empty of the love she remembered because her mother was gone.

In that respect, she did envy Daniel and his small family. At least they had each other. And she had—nobody—except the cousin whose life might be in danger at that very moment. She closed her eyes and her heart turned heavenward to plead for Maddie and anyone else who might be involved in this latest shooting. While she was at it, she also asked for clarity. Unless and until they figured out exactly what was happening and why, they might as well be wearing blindfolds and swinging wildly at invisible enemies.

She opened her eyes in response to a new radio dispatch.

"All units, suspect is believed to be driving a white older model car with a missing front bumper. He was last seen heading east on Fowler Street, crossing Main. Approach with caution. Suspect is armed."

Aurora leaned to peer out her window. "Fowler is up ahead."

"I know." She noted his hands fisted tightly on the wheel and his jaw set. "Hang on."

Daniel glanced in the mirror. "Dakota. Down. Stay."

To her temporary relief, Aurora saw the enormous dog obeyed immediately. Bracing with one hand on the dash and the other grabbing a handle above her door, Aurora pushed her feet hard against the floor as the SUV turned the corner onto Fowler. Main was only two blocks ahead.

A white car came barreling toward them with police cars in pursuit, lights flashing, sirens wailing, as nearby traffic pulled to the curb.

Daniel moved to the center of the street, slewed his armored SUV to take up most of the remaining room and stopped.

Aurora gasped. Everything was happening so fast she could

hardly think, let alone react logically. In spite of her seat belt tightening, Daniel threw an arm in front of her as if he hoped that would also protect her.

Eyes wide, she held her breath. The driver of the speeding car braked at the last second, sending his vehicle into a squealing skid and stopping with one corner of the protective push-bumper of Daniel's car denting his radiator.

Steam hissed. Men shouted. Armed officers were running toward the disabled white car as the driver's door opened and a scruffy-looking man tumbled out. He hit the ground running with Daniel and others in pursuit.

Oncoming traffic began crashing into the crumpled white vehicle and each other. Drivers were shouting in anger. An ambulance joined the fray, blocking traffic in the middle of Fowler and further tangling the mess of civilian cars and patrol vehicles.

Aurora got out, finding her knees a bit unsteady, and leaned against his SUV for temporary support. She had no idea where Daniel had gone or what his plans might be other than the fact he'd taken off without Dakota. The enormous K-9 was expressing her displeasure loud and clear too.

Easing around to the rear of the black SUV, Aurora patted the side window and spoke soothingly to the Dane. The volume of her barking lowered and Dakota seemed to be listening to her. "Easy. Easy, girl. He'll be back for us soon. I know he will."

Wagging her strong tail and circling, Dakota sidled up to the inside of the window while Aurora continued to try to calm her. "That's it. Good girl. Settle down."

Just as she thought her words were working, Aurora saw the K-9 stiffen, drop her front quarters to the floor and snarl against the glass. The effect was so startling Aurora jumped away…right into the arms of a man who looked exactly like the one who'd been at the courthouse trying to hurt Maddie.

He rasped, "Gotcha," as if pronouncing a death sentence.

Struggling and fighting to keep panic from disabling her, Aurora twisted in his grip, looked into his contorted face and shouted, "You have the wrong person!"

The assailant didn't release her immediately but he did stare in apparent disbelief so she added, "My name is Aurora."

"No. You're that DA. And you're gonna pay."

Out of the corner of her eye, she saw the hatchback begin to rise on its own. Before her captor had time to let go and run, Dakota jumped down and bit into his calf.

Of course! Daniel had a remote key fob that would release his K-9 from a distance. He must have seen what was happening to her and was on his way.

Head spinning, breathing ragged, Aurora sagged against the SUV as Dakota used both size and strength to overpower the man who had threatened her and held him down until Daniel ran up and gave the command to release.

Desperately wanting to hug both the agent and his dog, Aurora started with the one who was acting the happiest, bent and threw her arms around the neck of the brave canine.

Daniel gently urged her to rise and turned her to look at him. "Are you all right?"

"I—I think so."

"Why did you get out of the car?" He knew he sounded cross but seeing Aurora in such imminent danger had thrown his usually calm emotions into chaos.

"What did you expect me to do? Stay there like a sitting duck?"

"In a safe, bulletproof car, yes," he said firmly. Uniformed officers had handcuffed their prisoner and were escorting him away. "Can I trust you to stay here with Dakota while I go find out more?"

She didn't want him to go, even angry, but she forced herself to nod. "Go ahead. Now that the guy who thought I was Maddie is caught, I'm beginning to think I'll be much safer if I ditch you anyway and go back to driving my own car. The garage says the repairs are finished."

"Don't even think about it," he warned.

"Just make sure Maddie's okay."

"Will do."

Watching him walk toward the cadre of patrol cars, she was struck by how masterful he looked, how in charge of the situation even though he was only one of many participants. That was one trait she really admired about the man. He never wavered when doing the right thing, upholding the law and fearlessly facing criminals.

He flashed a thumbs-up almost immediately and was on his way back to her in less than two minutes. The smile on his face was enough to lift her spirits before he said a word.

He slid behind the wheel while one of the officers snapped pictures of the minor damage to his SUV. "Good news all around. Your cousin is fine and this guy we stopped is the one who put the bullet holes in her car while we were standing there."

"You're sure?"

"Positive. The bullets from the courthouse match. His name is Tucker Williams. He's one of the guys Maddie prosecuted and sent to prison. He's out on probation and wanted to get even. He'd tracked her car and when he saw you, he figured you were her."

"I tried to tell him who I was. Does this mean I'm in the clear? Nobody wants me dead?"

"That's how it's starting to look."

"What do you mean, *starting*? Am I safe or not?"

Daniel eased the SUV backward to disengage from the wrecked suspect vehicle and steered clear before answering. "There's just one little glitch."

"Well?"

"We suspect that Williams's gun is one of the ghost guns from the trafficking ring we're after."

"Meaning it has no serial numbers? That doesn't prove he's directly connected to the illegal guns. Almost anybody can buy parts and cobble something together now that there are instructions all over the internet."

Daniel shrugged. "Time will tell. In the meantime, you need to stay in protective custody, just in case."

"Phooey."

Chuckling, he turned back the way they'd come and continued toward the courthouse. "That's hardly a lucid argument."

"Since when have you taken anything I say seriously?" To her chagrin, Daniel's smile faded so she added, "I'm sorry. I'm just uptight and worried about Maddie and taking it out on you. I didn't mean it. Much."

"Not much, huh?"

"Well, maybe a little." Casting him a sidelong glance, she noted a quirk at the corner of his mouth. He might be slightly miffed but he wasn't really mad at her. Besides, he had a lot on his mind besides just her. Between his responsibility for running the task force and his terminally ill sister, he had to be on edge. Anybody would be, especially a person who took everything as seriously as Daniel did.

"After we see Maddie, I'll consider rethinking my conclusions," Aurora said. As far as she was concerned, that was a big concession. Her erstwhile guardian apparently disagreed.

"Let me put it this way, CSI Martin, you work for the Plains City Police Department and whatever your chief says, goes. The last time I talked to him, he agreed that you should be protected. If I have to protect you from yourself, I will. Period."

"Pulling my boss into this is unfair."

"Oh, really? You're acting as if you are just an ordinary citizen. Well, you're not. You're an active member of the justice system in Pennington County. Part of a group of organizations that take care of their own. That's not going to change just because you want to get rid of me. Are we clear?"

She managed to answer, "Yes," before the tears started to gather. He was absolutely right. She'd been behaving like a spoiled brat and she knew it. What in the world was wrong with her? Where had her camaraderie and team spirit gone?

Worse and more importantly, why had the sense of love and acceptance she treasured disappeared? This wasn't like her. She loved her job, her place in the police department, her fellow employees and the cops they supported.

Staring out the side window to keep Daniel from seeing how guilty she felt, she sniffled and swiped away silent tears. The truth behind her adverse reactions to his efforts to look after her was not simple. On one hand, she saw herself as totally independent and self-sufficient. On the other hand, she sometimes felt as if she was responsible for finding definitive clues to every crime and also holding her fractured family together in spite of everything that had happened to the contrary. Logic said those burdens were imagined, yet such thoughts threatened to crush her when she allowed herself to dwell on them.

The plain truth? She was accomplished and proud of her CSI skills, was well thought of at the PD and for the most part was satisfied with the way her personal life was playing out. She had friends and of course her cousin to rely on. The people she worked with could be counted on in emergencies too, just as Daniel was currently proving. All in all, she should be happy. And she was, most of the time.

Only one thing truly bothered her. Like it or not, when the door to her apartment closed every evening and she had quiet time in which to reflect, she could not escape the fact that she was lonely.

THIRTEEN

Maddie was already in the courtroom participating in the Derek Carlson trial by the time Daniel and Aurora arrived back at the courthouse. Jury selection was proceeding nicely.

Speaking aside to one of the armed guards at the door and displaying his badge, Daniel managed to convince the man to let Aurora peek in at her beloved cousin.

Sighing, satisfied, she stepped back and looked up at him. "Thanks. I needed to see for myself."

"I know." He didn't have to work to project tenderness. He felt it all the way to his core. Less than a year ago, he'd been unencumbered by any close family and here he was, actually feeling drawn to a young woman whose presence had softened his outlook almost as much as the prospect of becoming the adoptive father of a toddler.

In retrospect, Daniel could see that all the changes in his world had worked together. First Joy, then Serena and of course the beloved grandmother he had to call on for help with his new daughter. Catherine, *Nana*, had needed to express her love as much as Joy had needed to receive it. He could see that now. And Serena? Well, she'd needed all of them and still did. When it came time to bid her a final goodbye, he knew he was going to be deeply moved. It wasn't just what they had shared since she'd left her child with him; it was all the opportunities they had lost because of one man's selfishness.

Daniel gritted his teeth. Aurora had said she was disappointed in her own father. Well, he had plenty of animosity against his too.

Cupping her elbow, he escorted Aurora out of the courthouse and back to his SUV. Once they were seated comfortably inside and moving, he asked, "Do you mind going back to the station? I need to make arrangements to have this window repaired and see if I can borrow another car in the meantime."

She wrapped her arms around herself against the cold seeping through the fractured safety glass. "Sounds good to me. It's bound to either rain or snow soon. I can feel it."

Daniel had to smile. "Nana says she can predict changes in the weather better than the pros on TV. Aches and pains tell her."

"With me, it's mostly headaches," Aurora said, glancing over at him.

He met her gaze. "Do you have one now?"

"Not a bad one but enough to let me know barometric pressure is changing. It's a blessing and a curse."

"Lots of things are," Daniel said soberly. "It's good that we were able to ID and apprehend the shooter from the courthouse but that doesn't solve all our mysteries."

"Matching the ballistics to other incidents may help. We'll see. It would be helpful if we found a direct tie to your gun trafficking gang.

"True." Pausing while he negotiated the turn into the PCPD lot, Daniel continued, "However, considering all the choices of illegal firearms the gun traffickers have, I'm afraid it will be tough to match anything."

"True." Aurora sighed. "Does it ever seem to you as though we're beating our heads against a brick wall and it's not budging no matter how hard we hit it?"

"An interesting analogy given your headache. Yes. It does feel like that sometimes. The thing is, if we can find the tiniest crack in that wall we can exploit it and bring the whole structure crashing down."

"What would you say is going to make that crack?"

"It's hard to say. Maybe one of the minor players we already have in jail. Or maybe Brandon Jones—sorry, Murray—will make a mistake. He's not the sharpest pencil in the box."

Pensive, she nodded. "That's one of the details that's been bothering me. Hal was supposed to be the brains, yet their organization seems to be functioning just as well without him. What do you attribute that to?"

"Maybe a solid structure that Hal built while he was alive? I don't know. We really haven't heard reports of anyone else helping him plan, so I assume Brandon is following his brother's previous instructions."

"Which may mean that he'll eventually run out of wise moves and have to start thinking on his own. That's probably a good thing."

"Right." Parking, Daniel went to release Dakota while Aurora got out to wait for them. Although he was still wary and kept an eye on nearby activity, he was thankful to see his K-9 acting relaxed and calm. The dog's instincts were a lot sharper than those of a human, no matter how vigilant he was, and it gave him a good feeling to be able to rely on his canine partner.

Nevertheless, he motioned Aurora to start toward the rear entrance of the station and followed her. Other officers were coming and going. Patrol cars were moving slowly by. And there was enough activity to deter almost any would-be assassin. That was part of the problem with believing Brandon Jones/Murray was calling the shots now. He was a hothead. The kind of man who acted first and didn't consider the possible consequences until later. That made him dangerous. Unpredictable.

Waiting for him to enter the code to unlock the exterior

door, Aurora stood aside. "I still don't know why you keep insisting we have to stay together."

"Are you tired of my company? Dakota will be disappointed."

Preceding him inside, she spoke quietly. "It's not you. I'm just feeling a little claustrophobic with all the attention you're paying me. That Williams guy admitted to shooting Maddie's car and then trying to hit her again at the courthouse. He told me he thought I was her. I'm in the clear."

She had a point. Daniel nodded. "Okay. Let's agree you're out of danger from him. What about the guy who grabbed you outside your apartment? We never caught him or the ones that shot up Maddie's apartment."

"If the men you did arrest are sharing a lawyer, doesn't it stand to reason that they also share a connection to this Brandon guy?"

"Them, probably. Tucker Williams just admitted he was after Maddie so that's one down. We don't know enough about the rest."

"Meaning you still think I could have been their target? Isn't that stretching a bit?"

Logic told him she had a valid point. "Okay, let's say you're right."

"Gee, thanks."

"I'll rephrase that. I admit you have a good chance of being correct about the origins of our enemies. In some ways, that conclusion should help defer further attacks on you. There's only one problem that I can see."

Watching her hands fist and her jaw clench, he chose his words carefully. "It's your connection to me."

"What? We have no connection other than working out of the same building. We're not even on the same floor."

"Not at work. Here. Now. As the agent in charge, I have a target on my back too. Like I've said, the gang has targeted me and my team. We've all taken precautions. That won't end until we've captured the people at the top, namely Brandon and whoever he's using to replace Hal."

"Terrific. So, in other words, they think you and I are an item and that puts me right back in the fight."

"In a manner of speaking, I guess so."

"Then we're breaking up as of this minute," Aurora said. "If I have to stand in the town square and pretend to have an argument with you, I will. I'm tired of feeling like a prisoner without being behind bars."

"It's not that simple."

"Nothing ever is," she said with a grimace. "Seriously, what can we do?"

"Catch the bad guys, especially Brandon Jones/Murray, and dismantle the trafficking ring. We're putting plans in place to take down the whole organization. These other threats to you and Maddie have been a distraction and I can't help wondering if that's exactly what they were meant to do."

"Humph. Getting shot at is hardly a minor distraction."

"Compared to wiping out a criminal organization the size of the Murray operation, it is. Not to the victims, of course. I don't mean to minimize anyone's tragedy. I just mean we will save a lot of innocent lives if and when we get those hundreds of guns off the streets."

"The outlying areas especially are full of legally armed people. They always have been. They're not evil."

"I don't mean them. I'm talking about criminals getting their hands on illegal firearms and using them in the commission of lethal crimes. What the Jones/Murray gang is selling is death, period. Not personal protection. Death. There's a big difference."

Seeing Aurora nodding a response was comforting. Thankfully, she got it. She might not like the current circumstances but she definitely saw his point. That would suffice, for now.

And, when he and his team did finally end the trafficking in the Dakotas it would be one more step in the war against the tools of crime and those who got rich by supplying them.

The way Daniel saw it, all he had to do was protect Aurora, his team and their families, as well as his own, until the last detail of the final raid was in place, then act. He smiled slightly as his mind added, *And pray for success.*

Aurora had been back at her own desk in the lab for less than an hour when Daniel burst through the door. The first thing she noticed was his expression of deep concern. The second thing was the absence of Dakota.

Pushing her chair back, she stood. "What's wrong?"

"Serena," he said. "The hospice called."

"Is she…?"

Daniel shook his head. "No. But they want us all to come ASAP. She's looking and sounding better and singing modern Christian songs."

Puzzled, Aurora asked, "Is that bad?"

"Yes. They think it's a final rally before she lets go." He swallowed hard. "Will you come too?"

Even if he had not asked, Aurora would have volunteered to accompany him. She could see how much emotional stress he was under and her heart ached for him. And for the little girl whose mother was failing fast. "Of course. Anything I can do to help."

This time his reply was wordless but the glistening of his eyes and shaky breath revealed how deeply moved he was.

"What about Catherine and Joy? Are they on their way too?"

"Not yet. The Marshals left Nana without wheels so we'll go pick them up."

"In a car with a back seat, I hope," Aurora said, remembering having to cram into the agent's SUV with Maddie.

"Yes. I'm borrowing an unmarked patrol car while my broken window is being repaired. There'll be room for everyone."

Snatching up her jacket and shoving her phone into an inside pocket, Aurora started for the lab door. "Then come on. We don't want to be too late."

She'd had a brief experience with hospice when her mother passed and knew how accurately those nurses could predict someone's end. It was uncanny unless you actually asked about the signs. They weren't always the same of course, but they did follow a set of common patterns. Some of those were the steady stare at someone or something that was only visible to the patient. Another was a sudden sense of well-being as if a cure was in the offing, the way it had been with her own mother at the end. Although Aurora had never heard of a terminal patient actually singing, it made sense. After all, hymns were a form of worship so why not express those tender feelings during times of duress?

A dark blue sedan was waiting at the side door when she and Daniel left the station. An officer handed him the keys and wished him well. He slid behind the wheel while Aurora took the front passenger seat. She glanced back. "Won't we need a child seat for Joy?"

"Nana has one with her at the safe house that I'll install in this car. I just hope Serena is acting as happy as they said she was when we get there."

"My mother kept that last smile even after her heart stopped," Aurora said quietly. "It's one of the memories I cherish."

The look he shot her was so emotionally charged she chose to elaborate. "It's hard to explain. It seemed like a final gift, in a way. As if Mom was blessing me one last time."

"Then I hope Joy gets the same from Serena," Daniel said. "I don't think she understands what's going to happen."

"Not fully, no, but she's had enough time with you and

Catherine to know she's loved and has a home. I don't think she'll be nearly as sad as the rest of us."

"Us?"

Aurora blinked back tears and nodded. "Yes. Us. I don't know your sister well but I like to think we hit it off when we met. It's sometimes that way with believers. We have Jesus in common and He connects us. The Spirit connects us."

Although he kept his eyes on the road, she could tell he agreed when he said, "Maybe that's why Serena wanted you to come with me again."

"She did?"

"Yes. Nana was very clear about her wishes the last time we spoke. I didn't quite understand then but I think I do now. Serena felt the same connection you just described."

"Probably. It's pretty undeniable when it happens. Lots of people don't believe it because they haven't had the experience."

"Well, real or not, if it makes Serena happy in her last hours, it's fine with me."

Blinking, thinking, wondering, Aurora held her tongue. She wanted to ask him if he'd rather have left her behind, if he'd only included her for his sister's sake, but she bit back the words. What she, personally, felt at a time like this was of little importance. A young woman was nearing the end of her life and wanted to bid her family, her little girl especially, a loving farewell. The rest of the adults were there as mere observers. *And for prayers,* Aurora added. Especially for prayers.

FOURTEEN

Daniel slowly approached the safe house on Lowell where Catherine and Joy had been placed, cruising past the first time.

"Is it that one?" Aurora asked, pointing. "I think I saw the curtains move."

"Yes. I'm going to turn around and wait for a few minutes to be sure we weren't followed."

"Why would we be? Nobody knows what you're driving and I'm supposed to be out of danger."

"Except for your association with me and my team," Daniel reminded her. "There's still that."

"Maybe you're imagining more threat than there really is. I mean, Hal Murray is dead and you've got a couple of gang members in jail already. Why would they bother trying to harm DGTF members when that would call more attention to them? Aren't they mostly interested in smuggling illegal guns?"

"If Brandon wasn't a hothead, they probably would be," Daniel replied. "The thing is, we've had multiple reports of a vendetta. I'm not imagining the importance of the threat, Aurora. Look at the men we already caught trying to get into my place. They weren't there to sell cookies or magazine subscriptions."

"Okay, okay. I get it."

Keying his cell phone, Daniel contacted his grandmother. "We're here, Nana. Dark blue unmarked car. Can you see us?"

Catherine's answer was almost a screech. "That's *you*? Why didn't you say so sooner? I was about to call my handler and hide in a closet."

"Sorry. I needed repairs to my car and extra seating for you and Joy so I borrowed different wheels. Bring her car seat out with you. I'll meet you in the driveway."

"Do you want me to move to the back?" Aurora asked as he negotiated the turn and brought the car to a smooth stop.

"No. Stay where you are. Nana can ride in back with Joy and keep her occupied." Pausing, he smiled over at his passenger. "You can tell her more princess stories another time."

"It will be my pleasure," Aurora said, choking up.

Daniel felt a lump in his throat and his vision misted in response to her tender, heartfelt words. Their eyes met. "Thanks for coming with me, with us, today. If I had realized the similarity with your loss of your mother, I wouldn't have asked you."

"I'm glad you did," she replied, sniffling. "I think we go through trials in life for several reasons, one of them being the need to relate to others, later, and help them cope."

"Still, if you find it too difficult to stay in the room and deal with something that's too painful, please promise me you'll step out."

Her "I will," didn't sound very convincing but he let it go. What any of them did or didn't do when they were with Serena would just happen. All the planning and rehearsing in the world was not enough to carry the traumatic event they were likely to experience. He'd seen comrades fall and pass away in the line of duty but he'd never been involved in anything like Serena's lingering illness. Thinking back to what Aurora had said about shared experiences, he wondered if she believed that was why she'd become involved. It was a possibility that deserved consideration.

The way Daniel saw Serena's situation, he could either accept it or fight against it, and given his sister's obvious suffering and her unquestionable readiness to find eternal rest, it felt wrong to argue. The Bible said there was a time for everything. If this was the end of Serena's time, he'd be doing her a disservice if he railed against God for giving her peace at the end of her life.

Still, he didn't have to like it. All he had to do, really, was make things easier for little Joy so her last memories of her mother were good ones.

Having the opportunity to do that, or at least try, was God's gift to him, Daniel realized belatedly, partnered with Aurora's presence. That thought, that truth, settled in his heart and cloaked the rock of sorrow, padding its rough edges enough to allow him to function as necessary. The grief was real. So was the deep sense of comfort.

The four of them proceeded toward the hospital in silence. Aurora had greeted Catherine and Joy, continuing to smile as the other adults secured the toddler in her safety seat, but beyond that she didn't know what to say. Apparently, no one else did either. Even the usually loquacious child was quiet.

That silence continued as everyone piled out and waited inside the hospital lobby while Daniel parked. He was fisting the keys as he jogged up to join them.

They all turned toward the elevators. Aurora wondered if any of the others were noticing the antiseptic smell and the murmur of muted voices. This was not only a sad day for the Slater family, it was the same for many others and she imagined a sense of dread hanging over the whole building and making the air barely breathable. This was the adverse reaction Daniel had anticipated, she knew, yet she was determined to be strong for Joy. Perhaps that was why Serena had requested that she come too, she mused. Maybe the patient had sensed an inner strength that came from the Lord they both served. Aurora prayed it was so. She didn't want to color what might be Joy's last visit with her mama.

A large arrangement of real flowers sat on the tray table next to Serena's bed. Aurora hung back while Catherine carried Joy closer and Daniel backed them up, leaning in to pat his sister's shoulder affectionately. Everyone was smiling. Joy clapped her hands, no longer acting cowed by the hospital atmosphere. Catherine lowered her slowly to sit next to her frail mother just as Aurora had done on their previous visit.

Unwanted tears gathered in Aurora's eyes. Seeing this much love made her ache inside and want to experience the same thing; to go back in time and bask in the love her own mother had shared so openly, so beautifully.

The urge to leave the room and bury her personal feelings was strong. Her sense of duty and purpose was stronger and she was glad she was still there when Serena called her to come closer. Smiling, she sniffled, hoping nobody would notice how emotional she was becoming.

Serena's smile held love and promise as she reached for Aurora's hand. "I'm so glad you came again."

It seemed wrong to say it was a pleasure so she merely smiled back.

Serena's formerly pale cheeks seemed to blossom as she glanced aside at her child. "I want you to promise you'll be Joy's friend forever."

How could anyone refuse? "Of course. She's a very special girl."

The child seated on the bed looked back and forth between the two young women. "I'm a princess."

They both laughed through tears. "Of course you are," Serena said. "And all princesses have special helpers. Did you know that?"

"Uh-uh."

"Well, they do. And Aurora is going to be yours."

"Okay. When?"

"When I go to be with Jesus in Heaven," Serena said.

Aurora could tell what a struggle it was for the younger woman to contain her weeping and she was proud of the intense effort. She was proud of Serena, period. Not everyone approached the end of life on earth with such grace and assurance. Perhaps having had a year or better in which to come to terms with it had helped. And of course so had her Christianity. A believer didn't have to understand all the details to rely on God. That kind of universal wisdom wasn't accessible to mankind. But love and trust were. That was the truth cited in Scripture, the path that led to following Jesus.

Instead of the denial Aurora had expected, little Joy simply said, "Okay. I love you, Mama," and leaned to kiss her mother's tear-damp cheek.

It was an image Aurora knew she would carry with her and cherish for the rest of her life. A simple, pure love untainted by adult influence or doubt. She'd come to the hospital in order to give solace and had instead received a precious gift herself. No wonder Jesus had opened his arms to little children. They were the only ones capable of that kind of unrestricted love.

"I love you too, Princess Joy," Serena said. "And now I'm really tired. Will you go and let me take a nap?"

"Uh-huh. Night, Mommy."

"Good night, sweetheart."

Aurora watched Catherine start to lift Joy before Daniel stepped in and scooped her up, swinging her around as if playing a fun game and heading out the door. Catherine bent to kiss her granddaughter's pale cheek before gesturing to Aurora that it was her turn. A turn she didn't want, yet had to take.

Gently grasping the younger woman's thin hand, Aurora said, "I promise to do the best I can to help Joy."

"And you have no idea how you'll stay in touch, right?"

That surprised Aurora. "Well, I…"

"Don't worry about it. I have a feeling you and my brother will work something out. I can tell you have feelings for him."

"We just work together."

"Have it your way. I won't be here to play matchmaker but I want you to think of me every time you and Daniel meet, at least for a little while."

Aurora wanted to fully explain the connection between her and Daniel Slater and she would have if she hadn't been concerned about causing worry for Serena.

Leaning down, Aurora placed a kiss on Serena's forehead, noting that her skin felt cool and her eyes were now closed. The electronic monitors beside the bed continued to beep regularly, recording heartbeats and respirations, so Aurora knew Serena was still there. How long she would linger was a question no one could answer.

She straightened, looking to the nearest nurse. "Should we go or stick around, do you think?"

"Since she asked her daughter to go and let her rest, I think you should all do the same."

"But, what if…?"

"Sometimes patients wait for family to leave before they finally let go. Give her the peace she's asked for."

With that, Aurora turned and followed the others out the door, nodding at the officer guarding the door as she passed despite blinking back tears. *Peace? Oh, yes. That would be a wonderful gift for all of them.*

Daniel waited in the security of the hospice lobby with his grandmother and Joy. Even the usually chatty toddler was subdued, obviously picking up on adult moods, which was one reason why he'd avoided having in-depth conversations with his sister about her illness in front of the impressionable child. The only thing he could think to do at the moment was offer distraction, so he asked, "How about going for ice cream on the way home?"

Joy clapped her pudgy hands. "Yay! Ice cream."

"That's one vote in favor," he said, smiling at Catherine. "How about you? My treat."

"I'm really not hungry."

"What does that have to do with it?" Daniel teased. It took effort to properly deliver a quip but he managed, or so he hoped.

Seeing Aurora getting off the elevator, he whispered to Joy, then set her on the ground and let go. She headed for her storyteller friend at top speed for those short little legs and landed with a hug around Aurora's knees.

"Well, hello there." She grinned down. "Sorry to keep everybody waiting."

"We gonna get ice cream!" Joy announced.

"That sounds wonderful." Grasping one little hand, Aurora led the toddler back to Daniel and his grandmother as she asked, "What kind do you like?"

"Stachoo," Joy said loudly.

Watching the exchange, Daniel half expected Aurora to say, "Bless you," as if Joy had sneezed. Instead, she paused for a moment, then guessed, "The green one?"

Fine golden curls bobbed. "Uh-huh. Stachoo."

"Pistachio. I love that flavor.

Sighing, he added, "Yeah, me too."

"I'm glad you're loosening up a little," Aurora told him, smiling slightly. "You have so much on your mind besides work-related problems it's time you took a little time to relax." She paused, thoughtful. "Are you sure it's safe, I mean with everything else that's been going on?"

"I'll have a couple of my team members meet us there, just in case. We can't stop living just because we have enemies."

"So, does this mean you'll be letting me resume regular life soon?"

Daniel nodded, sobering and leading the way to the unmarked police car he'd borrowed. He was walking a fine line here and he knew it. It was impossible to provide the kind of total protection he needed for his loved ones without scaring them to death and perhaps mentally scarring Joy for life, as if she wasn't already going to be struggling to cope after Serena died.

Daniel shivered. Losing Serena was inevitable. He knew that. What he refused to even consider was the possibility of losing anyone else he held dear.

FIFTEEN

Aurora recognized several of the unmarked vehicles in the parking lot next to the ice-cream shop. Moreover, Beau was standing out front beside Jack and she thought she saw US Marshal Lorelei Danvers approaching the two with a big smile of greeting.

"This kind of spoils our being incognito but I'm glad to see backup."

"Better too many cops than too few," Daniel was quick to say.

"Can't argue with that." Feeling more at ease with at least two others and Beau on their side, Aurora led the way to the glass door into the shop while Daniel followed with Joy and Catherine brought up the rear.

Lastly, Jack held the door for Lorelei. Beau was at a tight heel. "Are we here to eat too," he asked Daniel, "or is this a work assignment?"

"You're all welcome to order whatever you like, even Beau, as long as he doesn't rat us out to Dakota the next time he sees her. She loves ice cream, especially in the summer."

"Is that why you picked this place now?" Aurora asked. "Because it's not as busy when the outside temps are the same as the freezers in here?"

"It's not *that* cold," Daniel countered. "Besides, they serve hot chocolate if you'd rather."

"I might."

"What about you, Princess?" He was holding her at an angle over the glass counter so she could look down on the tubs of ice cream. "There's your Pistachio. Would you like a scoop of that in a dish?"

She was nodding vigorously. "Yeah!"

Daniel placed their orders, then stood back and gave the others room while Aurora tended to Joy. After everyone was served and seated, he handed over his credit card.

Their party was the only group in the small ice-cream parlor and they took up two of the small round wrought iron tables. Aurora pulled Joy onto her lap so she could reach the table and feed herself.

Daniel joined them. "I can do that. You'll get all sticky."

"I don't mind." And she meant it. The sense of family she was feeling by letting the toddler sit in her lap was not only surprising, it was pleasing.

"Will you help her eat? She's not the best with a spoon."

"How will she improve if we keep insisting on doing things for her?" Aurora hadn't meant to be critical, but judging by the scowl on Daniel's face, he hadn't taken her comment well. Not that she intended to make any excuses. After all, she was right. Children, like everyone else, learned by doing. By observing. By hands-on experiences. She'd seen it happen time after time when she'd assisted in her mother's small day care as a teen.

"I think she's doing fine," Catherine added, smiling at the toddler as well as at Aurora. "We all are, considering the way our lives have gone lately."

At a different table, Lorelei put her spoon down. "So right, Mrs. Slater. I hope you're enjoying your stay at the new place."

Catherine smiled. "About the time I figure out where everything is stored we'll probably be on our way home but I'm not complaining. The important thing is keeping our special girl safe."

Joy beamed, slopping melting ice cream on the front of her jacket. "Oops."

Aurora wiped it off. "It's okay. I've got it."

Out of the corner of her eye, she saw movement. Jack, still seated with the marshal, had pivoted to face the door. Lying on the floor under the table, Beau shifted his attention too.

Seeing Daniel also adjust his chair, Aurora reacted in like manner. Soon, everyone except the toddler was staring across the room where a lone customer stood at the counter, apparently ordering. There was nothing notable about the man in the dark parka since that was pretty much the standard color for winter in Plains City. Only ski buffs wore bright clothing and it was too early in the season for many of those to have arrived.

As soon as the nearby hills had accumulated a good snow pack, little Plains City would be entertaining a quadrupled population until well after the first of the year. There had been some ski seasons, Aurora recalled, that had lasted well into spring. Everything depended on favorable weather, which in this case meant below freezing. Despite all the advantages to town prosperity, she was always glad when snowmelt filled the rivers and their influx of winter guests began to wane.

The man at the counter paid, took his cone in hand and paused to look around while he licked it. As his gaze passed over her closely grouped party, it didn't slow, yet she couldn't help shivering. The stranger hadn't said or done a single thing wrong so why was she suddenly feeling nervous? Moreover, why was almost everyone else sitting there motionless?

The atmosphere in the small storefront was so fraught she jumped the instant the man moved. Still tending to drips of ice cream, he used his free hand to pull a cell phone out of his pocket and raised it to study the screen. At least that's what she thought he was doing until Daniel stood, loudly ordered, "Don't," and she realized the stranger had been aiming it at them.

Pivoting, he dropped his cone into the trash receptacle by the exit, straight-armed the glass door and began to flee.

Daniel followed him as far as the door. Jack, with Beau at heel, dashed past on foot to pursuit. Aurora couldn't see how far they went but it couldn't have been far because Jack was back in seconds and conferring privately with his boss.

Nodding to Jack, Daniel turned to face the group. "Everybody. Finish your ice cream right away or bring it with you. We need to leave. Now."

Because Catherine didn't seem as befuddled as she was, Aurora asked, "What just happened? I didn't see a gun or anything."

"Not a gun. Worse, in our case," the older woman answered. "When he held up his phone I think he was taking our picture."

"And there would be no reason for that unless he was up to no good, right?"

"Right."

Gathering up Joy's ice-cream cup and a fistful of napkins, Aurora let the child down carefully and stood. "Okay, Princess. Time to go. I'd take my treat to share with Dakota but dogs can't have chocolate or they get sick."

"Get her some like Beau got."

"Another time," Aurora promised. "Right now we have to go."

"'Cause Daddy says?"

At first she thought Joy had said Danny. Then she realized the toddler was referring to her uncle as her dad, which he would be once the adoption was finalized. Touched and thrilled for Daniel, she looked to see if he'd overheard.

No doubt he had. He was standing there, frozen in place, with his slack jaw showing astonishment. She'd never heard him ask Joy to call him daddy but there it was. Loud and clear. And the effect it had on stolid, all-business ATF Agent Daniel Slater was profound.

Aurora broke the silence by speaking to him. "Can you carry her? I'll bring the ice cream and napkins."

Crouching slightly, Daniel opened his arms to the little girl who would soon be his daughter and she responded in kind.

"Watch for sticky fingers," Aurora warned. "I haven't had a chance to wipe her hands very well."

"Doesn't matter," Daniel said, starting toward the exit where Jack and Lorelei waited, flanking the door so they could cover the street in both directions.

One word, Aurora mused. One word from the innocent, loving little girl and the mountain had moved. Daniel Slater had accepted his new title with an open heart and was looking at Joy in a different way. The change was subtle yet telling. His *daughter* had become acceptable in any and all situations, even when she might not be perfect or have clean hands. Personal convenience had given way to the kind of love that erased flaws, that ironed out figurative wrinkles in relationships.

Blinking back tears, she carried Joy's cup and enough napkins to take care of any future spills and followed the others to their cars.

Catherine deferred to Aurora as Daniel fastened the toddler in a safety seat. "You can finish helping our princess," she said. "You're already sticky. I'll sit up front for a change if you don't mind."

"Of course not." She managed to get in, but found it difficult balancing the cup with the plastic spoon while trying to fasten her own seat belt, so Daniel circled the sedan and leaned in.

"Let me do that for you."

Embarrassed, awed by the closeness and keyed up by their flight from the seemingly safe ice-cream parlor, Aurora chuckled and raised the ice cream out of his way. "I'd argue with you if I had any other choice."

"Of course you would."

She could tell by the tone of his voice that he'd cracked a smile. The belt clicked. Daniel turned his face. They were so close she felt his warm breath on her cheeks. Time stopped for Aurora. Was he thinking what she was? Would he lean just those few inches closer and kiss her again? Is that what she wanted? Did she dare dream that someone like this would care about her in a personal way, accept her into his circle of special friends or more?

Joy's shrill demand broke the mood. "Ice cream!"

Recovering as Daniel backed out of the car, Aurora said, "Please. We say may I please have my ice cream."

"Okay. Peas."

"That will do for now," Aurora managed, still breathless from being so close to leaning forward mere inches and kissing Daniel whether he liked it or not.

For a moment, she forgot all about the danger and the man with the camera as an image of a smile formed in her heart and mind and with it came the conclusion that he would probably have liked it. She knew *she* would have.

By prior arrangement, they drove their cars out of the parking lot at intervals. Daniel and his party led while the others spaced themselves out in traffic behind him, ready to catch up and intervene if trouble arose. Every other car and truck was suspicious until proven otherwise. Every driver looked sinister, even the apparently blameless soccer moms and matrons out for a day of casual shopping.

He kept one eye on his driving while checking the rear-view mirrors as often as was safe and met Aurora's gaze in the center mirror when he looked behind them. "Everything okay back there?"

"Yup. Almost done eating and not out of napkins yet. Life is good."

Although he assumed Aurora was merely filling the silence

with conversation as a means to alleviate her nervousness, he had to agree with her in principle. Life, in general, was good. The problem was the unforeseen obstacles he kept encountering. Like becoming responsible for a toddler when he'd been solo for so long. In retrospect, he could see some things that had changed him for the better. Others seemed to point out how off-kilter he had been before.

He drove for a bit, noting that his grandmother and Joy were both dozing. Finally, he spoke to her. "I want your life to be good, Aurora. If it was in my power, I'd make everybody's easy and peaceful. Only I don't have that ability."

"You're trying. I know that. It's just…"

"Just what?" Once again, he met her gaze in the mirror and saw that she was moved almost to tears. "I guess I'm expecting too much from some of the people in my life."

"Like your father?"

She nodded and sighed. "Yes. I wish I understood how he can behave the way he is when my mother's passing was so recent."

"People grieve different ways. You throw yourself into your work when you need distraction. I'm the same." He paused to glance at his grandmother. "Catherine and I will soon have a loss to process and it will be our job to keep that loss from coloring the life of a certain P-R-I-N-C-E-S-S."

"I wouldn't worry too much. Children react differently than adults. You saw that already."

"I did. If she needs counseling later, we'll be sure she gets it." Hesitating before asking a question that had been nagging at him, he finally said, "What did you and Serena talk about when she sent the rest of us away?"

Even in the reflection, Daniel could see Aurora's cheeks growing pinker. "Maybe later," she said as she cocked her head toward the little girl.

"Okay. I get it. When you're ready, we can talk. I want to

follow my sister's wishes as closely as possible, including adopting Joy. Serena deserves far more than she's ever gotten from my side of the family."

"I'm thankful she had the courage to reach out to you. You're going to be a great father."

Daniel didn't know what to say so he stayed silent. In his recent prayers, that was a paramount topic. The parenting example he had to follow was far less than ideal, so he'd made up his mind to reinvent the concept of fatherhood and family, giving it the same kind of dedication he gave his job.

Now that it was certain he would be adopting and raising his niece, he also knew how important it was that he not be taken from her the way her mother was about to be. Joy deserved a stable home, a place where she could blossom and grow to be a woman her mother would be proud of.

The muted ringing of his grandmother's cell phone drew him from his reverie. Trembling, she answered. Daniel's hands fisted on the steering wheel when he saw her expression changing. Bad news had brought tears to her eyes and her lower lip was quivering.

Before he could ask, Aurora did. "Serena?"

Catherine nodded sadly. "Yes. It's over."

"Is there anything I can do?" Aurora's voice was soft, tender.

"Yes," Daniel replied, again looking back at her reflection. "You can explain again and make sure our favorite member of royalty is okay."

"She will be," Aurora assured him. "It's the adults who will have trouble accepting anything other than healing. They always do."

"I know. And I agree. It seems so unfair."

"To us, it does. How does that Bible verse go? *For my thoughts are not your thoughts, neither are your ways my ways, saith the Lord.* I think it's in Isaiah."

Daniel took a few moments to sort his own thoughts before he replied. "Something just occurred to me. I'm glad you're here right now. You've brought what we need, what Joy needs, at exactly the right time." He coughed to cover his emotion. "Thank you."

He wasn't sure whether or not Aurora replied because there was a sudden whoop from a siren behind them. The radio sounded off. It was Jack. "Watch your flank. A speeder just passed me over a double line. Black pickup. Dakota plates. He's heading straight for you."

Random thoughts and musings were instantly erased from Daniel's mind and he was totally task-focused. His grip on the wheel tightened. His jaw clenched. He shouted, "Hang on!"

Milliseconds later, the sedan was hit on the rear fender and nearly shoved off the road. Skillful driving was all that kept them from hitting parked cars.

Accelerating out of danger gained Daniel very little time in which to maneuver. He could see flashing lights and hear sirens behind them. Backup was coming. Would it arrive soon enough?

To the women's credit, neither of them screamed. Catherine hunkered down in her seat. Aurora? She had thrown herself across the little girl next to her and was using her own body to shield the child.

Daniel tensed for a second hit. "Hang on. Here he comes again!"

This time, he was braced for the collision but that didn't change the way the SUV behaved in a skid. He alternated between brakes and accelerator to help even out their ride and pulled ahead. Seconds more. That was all he needed. Just a few more moments upright and intact before the patrol cars and some of his team caught up and took out their adversary.

Lights flashed behind and approached on his left. He slowed for safety and to give the officers time to maneuver around their pursuer. Instead, the truck sailed on past with two police cars in pursuit as Jack and Lorelei also gave chase.

Traffic had parted and thinned, giving him room to pull over when he was certain the last of the danger had passed.

Once he had radioed a report of their status, he relaxed enough to turn and look directly at Aurora. She was still leaning over Joy so he told her, "It's okay. We're in the clear now."

Long hair masked her cheek as she peered at him. "Promise?"

"Promise," he said. "I don't know how to thank you."

As she straightened and pushed back her hair, she paused to look at her fingers, then smiled slightly. "You can start by taking me home so I can wash my hair. There's green ice cream in it."

"Bravery in battle has its costs," Daniel quipped. He was so relieved that they were all okay he was almost giddy.

Turning back to drive, he paused to key the mic when dispatch reported that the suspected hit-and-run driver had escaped. That settled it. He was not taking Joy and his grandmother back to the safe house. Not when his substitute ride had been identified already.

"Change of plans," he announced flatly. "We're all going back to my house."

To his surprise he heard cheers from both the front and rear seats.

SIXTEEN

Aurora and Catherine took Joy upstairs with them. The older woman bathed the toddler while Aurora rinsed stickiness out of her hair. She was combing through tangles when Joy appeared, fresh faced and dressed in clean jammies, and climbed onto her lap.

Catherine lingered in the doorway. "Do you have everything you need?"

"I'm making do. It will be nice to go home again." She smiled over at her hostess. "No offense meant. I just like my cozy little apartment."

"This place can grow on you," Catherine said. "It has me. I told Daniel that as long as he hires help for cleaning, I'll be happy."

Smiling down at the little girl who was gently stroking her damp hair, she realized how much it must remind her of Serena's. That led to memories of the news she'd been asked to break. Her gaze locked on Catherine's and unspoken understanding passed between them.

Aurora faced the vanity mirror and saw their two faces reflected, one above the other, as if posing for a family portrait. She leaned closer to kiss the top of Joy's head.

"Remember how I told you about your mama going to Heaven?"

"Uh-huh."

"Well, after we saw her the last time, she went."

"Oh." The little blue eyes widened. "I can't go see her any-more?"

"No, honey. I'm sorry. We can't."

"Mommy was real sick. She said."

"Yes, she was. And now she won't hurt or be sick anymore."

Joy's lips pursed and she looked at Aurora in the mirror. "That's good, huh?"

"Yes. Very good."

"Don't be sad." Wiggling around, the toddler reached for Aurora's cheek and wiped away a tear. "It's okay."

Pulling her into a full embrace and holding her close, Aurora said, "Yes, Princess. It's very okay."

Daniel was in the lower level conducting a video confer-ence when he heard Joy's laughter with overtones of Aurora's sweet voice in the background. He felt his pulse jump. There was no denying that telling reaction. It was pure emotion and unfortunately quite unsettling, particularly since he'd heard Aurora say more than once that she was anti-marriage. For that matter, he'd done the same and just because he was mel-lowing, it didn't mean she was. After all, they would only be keeping company for a few more weeks at the most.

That conclusion helped him focus on the video conference he'd called, admitting the last participants with a click of his computer mouse.

"Can you hear me okay?" he asked to the group.

Heads bobbed. "All right," Daniel began. "I have an an-nouncement to make."

"Condolences," Jack said.

"Thank you but this is not about my sister." His grand-mother would be handling the funeral arrangements and he'd be sure to let his team know. "We need to wrap our heads around this upcoming operation. It's going to take coordina-

tion between the ATF, our team, local officers and the FBI."
He singled out one participant. "Lorelei, you will be in charge
of notifying the Marshal's office and making sure all our witnesses are safe and secure."

Lorelai nodded. "I understand you have CSI Martin and
your family with you. Will that arrangement continue?"

"I expect it to, at least until we're ready to make our big
move on the Murrays." He changed focus. "Jack, has there
been any additional info? We need more details about the next
shipment and who's on the receiving end."

"Copy, Daniel. My CI tells me he's sure this is going to
be the biggest transfer yet. Maybe all of the remaining stock.
He says he's been hired to drive one of the trucks and knows
there are at least two more involved."

"How big are we talking here?"

"Not semis," Jack said. "Think box trucks. Like the kind
people rent to move furniture."

"Got it. Did he say where they were staging?"

"Yes, and no. The one he's supposed to drive is already in
Plains City. Others are due to arrive, empty, from Fargo and
Rapid City. Once they're all in place and loaded, a convoy
will start north."

"Destination?"

"Unknown," Jack said, sounding disgusted.

"All right. We'll go with what we have. Lucy, check with
any informants you have in Fargo and see if you can get a line
on the incoming trucks."

"Copy," Lucy said, looking happy to have a specific task.

Daniel went on. "You and Kenyon will stand by with your
K-9s and wait for further orders."

He concentrated on the sheriff's deputy from Keystone,
Zach Kelcey and Detective West Cole from Plains City PD.
"Zach and West, you two worked together at Mount Rushmore
so you'll partner for this operation too. I want you to stage

with me when the time comes. Liam will be in reserve and I hope we won't need Guthrie for victim searches. Jenna, your home turf is Fargo too. If the convoy heads there, I'll want you to liaise with Lucy and their local PD. Otherwise, you'll be with me too. Any questions?"

"I'm good," Zach replied. "Just say when."

"Me too," Liam said. "As much as I like working Guthrie, I hope we don't have to search for more bodies this time."

"Affirmative," Daniel said formally.

Jack Donadio piped up. "What about me and Beau?"

Making a decision that he knew was colored by personal preference, Daniel hoped it wouldn't come back to bite him. "I'd like you and your K-9 to stay at my place until we're sure this operation is a go. After that, I'll revisit your placement."

It almost sounded as if Jack had moaned but if he did, he covered it well, although Daniel did see his shoulders shrug. "Okay. In the meantime, do you want me inside your house or out on patrol?"

"You can stand down and relax as long as Dakota and I are home," Daniel replied. "Just make yourself available at a moment's notice. We'll arrange a room for you." He could tell that Jack wasn't happy about the protection detail and, yes, he could have chosen someone else, but Jack not only knew the people he would be guarding, he was familiar with the Slater house. That gave him a big advantage over anyone from the outside.

"Okay," Daniel said soberly. "That's it for now. Make sure you and your dogs are rested and pack extra supplies in case we're on stakeout for an extended period."

"Is there a chance of that?" Jenna Morrow asked. "If so, I should notify my chief in Cold River."

Daniel shook his head rapidly, his brow knit. "No. Nobody outside our immediate circle is to know how close we are to ending this trafficking operation. Not even other law enforcement. If explanations are necessary, I'll make them myself. That goes for you too, Lorelei. You can tell your people that we need continued private access to the safe house we were using but nothing more. Understand? Same goes for whoever is watching our ADA, although I think her problems were solved when we arrested Tucker Williams."

Pausing to allow responses, Daniel studied each face. Members of his team were special in many ways and so were their K-9 partners. "I appreciate every one of you more than you know. Make whatever preparations you need to and stand by for further orders."

"How soon?" Jack asked.

"As soon as Brandon and his followers gather and prep to move north," Daniel said. "I expect that news to come at the last minute, so keep your radios on and cell phones charged."

Mics keyed and heads nodded as the team agreed.

"I know I picked the right people when I chose you and your dogs," he told them. "This hasn't been an easy road for the past eight months. Once we tie it up, you're all invited to my place for a party." Thinking about having his whole team together to celebrate made him smile. "If we finish this job before Thanksgiving, we'll have turkey with all the trimmings."

That said, Daniel's most fervent prayer was that they would all be alive and well to attend. Facing down the Jones/Murray gang was fraught with danger, particularly since Brandon was known to be mentally unstable.

As he ended the video conference, Daniel thought of God and prayed for all their safety, realizing as he did so that he had also constantly prayed for Serena's healing. It was hard to accept results contrary to his wishes, yet in retrospect he could see hidden blessings in her passing. Pain was gone. Suffering was over. Serena was loved and happy and secure. It was the rest of them, the ones she had left behind, who were sad and suffering.

Perhaps that was a gift too, he reasoned. Not everyone was missed and remembered fondly. It would be much, much sadder to leave this earth without anyone caring. Without anyone grieving your loss.

It took monumental effort to shake himself loose from his maudlin thoughts. The arrival of Dakota in the control room helped immeasurably. She galloped down the stairs and into the office space like an uncoordinated pup without a brain in her head, paused to slurp his arm from wrist to elbow, then plunked down in the bed he kept there for her and began to chew a hard rubber toy.

"You slobber too much," Daniel said with a chuckle. "I need to teach you to wipe your chin."

A soft chuckle came from the stairwell. He knew exactly who was there. "Aurora. Did you get the ice cream washed off okay?"

"Yup." She stepped into view clad in a gray sweat suit that was miles too big for her and spun in a circle. "See?"

Dampness darkened her blond hair and her freshly scrubbed cheeks made her look even younger than usual. The effect was a bit off-putting. Age might be relative once adults reached a certain maturity but he couldn't help thinking of how many years separated them.

"You look about ten years old in that outfit," he said, intending to make the observation sound like a joke.

Aurora fisted her hands on her hips. "Oh, yeah. Well you look ancient and moody when you scowl like that. Aren't you afraid you'll scare Joy?"

"Am I scaring you?" he asked before thinking.

"Hmm." She considered him with her head cocked to one side like a curious pup. "Naw. I guess not. You're entitled to have your moments." Sobering, she added, "When I told Joy about Serena, I think she took it really well. Catherine agrees. She can reassure you if you're still worried."

"Actually, I'm not," Daniel said. "I've heard you relate to Joy before. You're a natural with kids."

"When I was younger, I considered becoming an elementary school teacher. But by the time I'd had a taste of law enforcement, even though I washed out as a cop, I knew what my career path had to be."

"Well, if you ever decide to do something else, you'd make a great teacher."

"Thanks. Some kids are easy to like. Easy to relate to."

"I think I do better with dogs."

"And adults? Maybe, but that doesn't mean you can't learn. The thing I try to remember when I'm talking to kids is to not underestimate them. Don't talk down to them. They're a lot smarter than we give them credit for. We just need to be honest and avoid big words."

"And complicated theology? Yeah, I can see that. Your explanation was way better than mine. Joy got it right away."

"Perhaps whatever you said prepared her," Aurora suggested. "Same for Catherine. By the time I arrived, Joy was curious and ready for more. Sometimes I think God works that way."

"What way?" He busied himself straightening his desk to keep from having to make eye contact when his emotions were so heightened.

"One step at a time. Look back on this past year. You're not the same man you were when Serena left Joy outside the station with a note pinned to her. And I'm not the same CSI you knocked out of the way of those bullets either."

"You're not? How so?"

Chuckling softly, she shook her head and chose a chair near Dakota, reaching down to stroke the Dane's broad head between the ears. "Let's leave that discussion for another time. A quieter time. I heard some of what you were saying as I came down the stairs. How long do you think it will be before you can tighten the net around the traffickers?"

"They have to make the first move," he said, frowning again. "Forget anything you overheard, okay? That information is classified."

Aurora drew finger and thumb across her lips as if pulling an imaginary zipper. "Promise. Besides, I didn't hear any details so there's nothing to blab."

"I don't worry about that with you," Daniel assured her, "I just don't want you to be overly involved when you don't have to be. The less you know, the safer you are."

"Well…" She drew it out. "There is such a thing as being too ignorant. If you had told me in the first place that there was a vendetta against your team, I might have behaved differently."

"Oh? How? Would you have stayed away from me? Not lingered at the murder scene to be sure Miss Effie got protection? Not let me knock you down to save your life? Not stuck with me after we were targeted again and again?"

She struck a pose, the fingers and thumb of one hand coming together at the point of her chin, head tilted quizzically. "Hmm. Interesting questions."

"I thought so." A twitch at the corner of her mouth betrayed her true mood. A slight smile followed. That was enough to satisfy Dan.

He was just beginning to relax and feel back in control when she added sweetly, "So, are you going to take me with you on the raid?"

"Seriously?" He gaped. "Not in a million years."

To his surprise, she grinned and didn't argue. That casual reaction worried him almost as much as her suggestion that she be present for the takedown. He'd sooner drag his own grandmother along than include Aurora Martin.

SEVENTEEN

The next few days dragged by for Aurora. Daniel and Jack and sometimes even Catherine would stop talking the minute she tried to join their conversation, as if she was some kind of spy for the opposition. She knew they didn't think that of course, but it did hurt to be closed off when she truly wanted to be included. Granted, it wasn't safe for her to return home just yet. Not when the trafficking ring had her picture and could target her to get to Daniel and the DGTF. Still, it nettled her.

Nights were the worst. The house was so quiet it was almost creepy. Once Joy had been put to bed and Dakota had settled next to her, there were no sounds except for the hum of a digital clock on her bedside table and the occasional muted announcement from a police scanner in Catherine's room. With the older woman's bedroom door closed, Aurora had to strain to make out what was being said and a lot of what she did hear needed interpretation because it was incomplete.

Moreover, for no apparent reason she had begun sleeping lightly and listening for Joy. Any sounds of distress or need jarred Aurora awake and she often got up to tiptoe in to check on the toddler. Fortunately, Dakota knew her well enough by now to allow the occasional peek without alerting and waking the whole household.

This particular night however when something roused Aurora, she wasn't sure what she'd heard. Why was her heart pounding? She held her breath. Listened. At first, she thought perhaps she'd been dreaming but in a few moments she heard footsteps in the hallway. Murmured voices. A rustling as if something or someone was moving in the distance.

Her first instinct was to wait and see what developed. That notion was quickly overridden by the maternal urge to check on little Joy. Rising, she padded barefoot to the door of her room, entered the hall and made her way to the child's bedroom.

Sighing when she saw the fair hair on the pink pillow and the familiar lump beneath the quilt, Aurora was about to go back to bed when she noticed something extremely worrying. Dakota wasn't lying next to the bed!

So where was she? Why had she abandoned her post when she'd always faithfully guarded the sleeping child? Torn about whether to stay with Joy or look for the K-9, Aurora decided to wait there. If the canine returned, fine. If she didn't, then somebody needed to be looking after this helpless child.

It did occur to Aurora that she was unarmed and as such would be nearly helpless if an attack did come. But what kind of weapon could she find in the room of a twenty-two-month-old? Teddy bears weren't exactly lethal and children this young didn't play baseball so there was no bat to swing, not even a plastic one.

A long shadow fell across the doorway. Aurora stood her ground, placing her body between the sleeping girl and whatever danger might be looming. A face peeked around the jamb.

"Ah, there you are," Catherine said with a slight smile. "I thought we'd lost you too."

"Too?"

When the older woman entered the bedroom, Aurora was surprised to see a holster belted at her waist. The image was rather incongruous, considering her age, small stature and drooping blue terry cloth robe.

Catherine came closer and spoke in a whisper. "The others have left for the takedown. Daniel said it was safe enough as long as one of us was armed and all the doors and windows were locked. He figures the whole gang will take part in this transfer of the cases of guns because intel says they're not planning to come back here."

"The whole operation is leaving South Dakota?"

"Plains City, at least," Catherine said. "Maybe the whole area. He's afraid if they get away successfully and manage to set up in a new place, they'll be even harder to track down. That's why he took everybody on his team with him."

Aurora shivered. "Even Jack?"

"Yes. The informant is one of Jack's contacts and he'll need to make a positive identification. They've promised the guy immunity from prosecution. That won't do him any good if he's killed in the raid."

"I guess that makes sense." She glanced at the sleeping child. "I don't like being this exposed though."

"Neither do I." Resting her palm on the grip of her holstered gun, Catherine frowned. "What do you say you grab your boots and we move into the downstairs control room where we can watch the monitors in case there are more prowlers? Daniel didn't think there would be because we still have a police unit standing by outside but nobody's perfect."

"Right. Better safe than sorry."

Catherine chuckled. "My mama always used to say that."

"So did mine." Sobering, Aurora quickly slipped bare feet into the fur-lined boots in her room, grabbed her coat then returned.

"You carry the princess while I bring her quilt, jacket and a few toys for later," Catherine said. "I've already restocked drinks and snacks in the fridge down there. We could hold off an army if we had to."

"Let's hope and pray Daniel is right and we won't have to," Aurora said.

"And pray for him and his team."

"Amen. Here. Give me the jacket, she's shivering." Aurora dressed Joy, held her tight and headed for the bedroom door. This was not the scenario she had envisioned. Not even close. They were supposed to be safe there, not locked in an underground room with only one gun between them and the possibility of having to wait for hours—or longer—before they got word it was safe to come out.

The hallway was dark. Shafts of reflected light peeked in from outside where floodlights illuminated the landscaping. It helped to know Catherine was right behind her. Once they were locked in the office/control room, they'd be fine. Just a few more minutes, a few more steps.

A gasp broke the silence. Aurora whirled. The pink quilt Catherine had taken off Joy's bed was now held firm around her head and she was struggling to free herself from a masked man's grasp.

Help her? No, protect Joy, Aurora decided in the split second she had in which to make a move, torn between the two options. There was no time to think, no time to make a rational choice. As far as Aurora could see, there was only one right one. She had to escape in order to protect the innocent little girl she held in her arms. It was what Catherine and Daniel would want. But, oh, how she wanted to leap on the attacker and rip the older woman from his grasp.

There had to be a way. Only there wasn't. Not given the current circumstances. She couldn't save them all, just as the best doctors couldn't save Serena. Sometimes you had to choose the better of two unacceptable options and pray you were making the right decision.

Hurrying ahead, Aurora ran down the stairs, nearly tripping as she reached the bottom, then swung around the corner toward the metal door to Daniel's home office. It was closed. Keypad locked. And Catherine alone knew the code.

There was only one other place to go. The garage. By this time, Joy had awakened and was babbling about Dakota and ice cream and goodness knows what else. Aurora didn't have time or breath to reply. She freed one hand to jerk open the exterior door, although where she would go from there was an unknown.

Behind her, Catherine's protests were muted. In front lay the empty garage. One door yawned open. And in the yard just beyond the automatic door a black car was waiting. A dark figure emerged from the clouds of mist coming from the muffler as the car idled, ready, and purposely stepped over the prone body of a uniformed police officer.

Her heart leaped. That wasn't Daniel. Or Jack. But somebody was hurt. Aurora clutched Joy closer, wishing she'd gone back to try to free Catherine so they'd have some way to defend themselves since Catherine was the one with the gun.

She turned and realized that the thug who had captured Catherine in the quilt had joined them.

The man in the mist waved a gun. "Run and you all die."

It was too late.

Joining his contingent of the strike team, Daniel made sure everyone was on the same page for their plan before taking the time to call home. To his dismay, Catherine didn't answer her phone. He tried Aurora's number. Same problem. He called the station and asked to be patched through to the officers on duty outside his house. That call, too, went unanswered.

Jack tapped him on the shoulder. "What's up?"

"I'm not getting an answer at the house."

"I wouldn't worry about it. Catherine said she was probably going to gather everybody downstairs in your office so they could monitor the yard."

"They should be able to get a cell signal down there."

"Maybe they're sleeping." He yawned. "Like any normal person would be at this hour."

"I don't like it," Daniel insisted. He punched in the number of the Plains City PD and identified himself when dispatch answered.

"Yes, sir. How can we help you?"

"I can't raise the unit on duty at my house. I need a second car to go by make sure everything's secure," he said, explaining the reason for his concern.

"Will someone meet the arriving units?"

"No. I don't expect them to be able to rouse anyone inside unless they use the intercom on the gate. Once they get there and speak with my family, please let me know they're all right."

"Will do."

Ending the call, Daniel looked to the team member he now considered a friend. "I suppose you think I'm being overprotective about this but I can't help it."

"Nothing wrong with caring," Jack said. "It's pretty evident that the women in your family have you wrapped around their little fingers."

"I beg your pardon?"

Jack laughed. "You heard me. Catherine mothers you, Joy gets ice cream whenever she wants it and—" He broke off.

"And?"

"And, I've seen the way you look at Aurora Martin when you don't think she's aware. Why don't you just break down and admit you've got a thing for her?"

"She's a colleague."

"True. What else is she—or could she be?"

"I don't know what you're talking about."

"Hah! Maybe you can fool her, and even yourself, but your

grandmother and I have seen the truth and we agree. There are sparks every time you two meet."

Daniel gritted his teeth. Was it that obvious? Moreover, had he been kidding himself about his feelings? Perhaps, although nothing had happened that was powerful enough to cause him to rethink his sensible plans for the future. He already had the necessary elements of a core family. Joy had him and Catherine. She didn't need Aurora to be happy, nor did he.

That conclusion didn't sit quietly in his mind. Thoughts that eliminated Aurora's presence were unsettling to the point of excess nervousness. Pacing, he drove a fist into his opposite palm. This was not the time or the place to let his mind wander. The operation against the Jones/Murray gang called for a clear head. Something he had prided himself on in the past.

This was what happened when people let emotions lead them, Daniel reminded himself. He was above that. Or at least he always had been—until now.

The earbud that kept the task force's radio connections quiet sounded off and made him jump. He looked to Jack to make sure he too had received and understood the communication. A convoy of three trucks had just pulled out of the bay doors of the targeted warehouse. The guns were on the move.

This was where his opinion differed from that of local law enforcement. They wanted to stop the trucks, confiscate the guns and arrest everyone on scene. ATF felt that they'd accomplish more if they allowed the shipment to proceed to its destination where another contingent of the gang waited to receive them. His agency had prevailed, with caveats. There would be unmarked vehicles waiting to join a covert pursuit depending on road traffic and where the convoy was at dawn. Night would aid the police. Daylight would pose more problems.

With a nod to his partner, Daniel put Dakota into the rear of his repaired SUV and got behind the wheel. Jack was driving separately, giving them more of a variety of pursuit vehicles. One car would appear to drop out as another took its place, a version of police leapfrog. With enough cars in reserve, they'd be able to stay unseen as long as necessary. At least that was plan A.

Motor running but headlights off, Daniel was about to pull out from behind the bushes where he'd parked when he heard someone shout over his earpiece. "Car approaching from the east."

Daniel quickly keyed his mic. "All units, hold your positions."

Clicks of confirmation were his unspoken answers. Nothing moved except the strange black sedan that had appeared next to the lead truck in the procession. A slight figure clad all in black was getting out, waving both arms and walking toward the warehouse door. Whoever it was, they weren't part of his plans.

Seconds ticked by. There was clearly an argument going on next to the loaded trucks. He could even hear echoes of distant shouts although it was impossible to make out what was being said.

Finally, the original driver plodded back to the sedan and got in. Daniel trained binoculars on its windows. Backlit by the bright overheads mounted on the warehouse, he could make out shadows. Moving shadows. People? There were others in the car besides the driver? Brandon Murray, maybe?

"If that car separates from the convoy, keep it in sight," Daniel ordered. His cell phone buzzed. Recognizing the number, he was flooded with intense relief. "Nana."

The person who laughed wryly wasn't Catherine. "Good guess, cop. She's right here."

Gripping his phone tightly, Daniel was at a loss. The caller sounded female but unlike anyone he could recall. "Who are you? Where's my grandmother?"

"Like I said, right here with me. We had a nice ride, didn't we folks?"

"Ride?"

A laugh cackled. "You're even denser than I thought. I know you're out there, watching us. That's exactly where I want you. I got to see Hal die and I'm going to return the favor." More unhinged laughter sounded. "Before I leave town, I'm going to let you watch your family disappear, one at a time, starting with…"

There was a pause and Daniel could hear weeping in the background. Then he heard a high-pitched wail and his resolve fractured into a thousand pieces. It was Joy.

EIGHTEEN

Listening to the horrid conversation and seeing the barrel of a gun swinging toward them, Aurora threw her body across the frightened child and shouted, "No!"

Catherine made a lunge for the hand holding the pistol and it went off with a bang that rattled the car windows and left Aurora's ears ringing. Thankfully, the bullet had gone wild and left a hole in the car windshield, not in one of them.

She didn't know where Daniel and his team were in relation to the car but judging by the way their captor was talking to him, this must be the warehouse his team had been looking for. Moreover, since the bitter gray-haired woman had threatened to make him watch what was happening, he had to be close by. That conclusion did help calm her a little. Being held at gunpoint however did not. Part of her wanted to mimic Catherine and leap on the kidnapper while another part was barely able to think, let alone act.

Joy was sobbing. Aurora held her tightly and prayed almost incoherently, hoping God would listen to her heart, not her jumbled words. Some of her most powerful prayers had been like that. Tears rather than eloquence.

Clearly, plans had to change, Aurora decided. Daniel had told her that they intended to let the gun shipment continue so they could arrest all the criminals at the arrival site. Given the current circumstances, that wasn't likely.

Concerned only for their survival, she refused to worry about anyone's clever plans. All Aurora cared about was getting out of this mess alive and seeing her innocent companions saved as well. Later, if Daniel wanted to berate her for fouling up his operation, she'd be more than willing to listen and accept whatever blame he chose to assign.

Right after I tell him I love him, she added silently. If anybody could get them out of this, Daniel Slater could. *With the help of God?* Yes, she didn't have to know how; she simply trusted him. Them. Faith was funny like that. Knowing a rescue was possible and believing there would be a heroic attempt to affect it, she was able to imagine a happy ending to this terrible dilemma. Some people might accuse her of being foolish, as some had in the past. But she had seen amazing, impossible things happen before and there was no reason to doubt they could happen again.

Aurora's musings took her to Serena's passing. That had been an answer too, in a way, although it was hard to accept that earthly healing didn't take place whenever it was asked for. As she had told Joy, Serena was out of pain and healed in another way, a way that humans dreaded.

"I don't want to be done yet," she whispered.

Catherine overheard and leaned close to reply very quietly. "Me either, kiddo. Trust my grandson. He'll get us out of this."

"He'd better," Aurora said, managing a slight smile. "I have something important to tell him."

A maniacal cackle from the driver's seat sent shivers down her back. When their captor said, "Lots of luck living that long," an icy cloak of terror wrapped around Aurora, causing her to pull Joy even closer and tuck her inside her coat as if that would help protect her.

"Shots fired!" Daniel had bailed out of his car, leashed his K-9 and joined Jack in a crouch next to their vehicles. Both

Beau and Dakota were wearing bullet-resistant vests, as were the human members of the team.

"They have to be over there," Daniel said, pointing. "I heard the gunshot over the phone at the same time it blasted through that car."

"Agreed. How do you want to proceed?"

For the first time in memory, Daniel regretted being in charge. It was his duty to stop the gun trafficking, yes, but he also had a duty to protect human life. Knowing that his loved ones were in danger changed the dynamics of the situation in ways he didn't like to think about. Ideally, he'd be able to stop the trucks as well as rescue the kidnapped victims. How he was going to do that was the big question. He had no idea.

There was no time for serious prayer so he merely glanced at the night sky and mouthed, *Please.* That would have to suffice, and he knew in his heart that it would. If he'd learned anything lately, it was that God could be trusted even when a person didn't understand divine decisions. He also believed that there was nothing wrong with asking for deliverance, one way or another. Just because he might not see a way out of this current trap, didn't mean there wasn't one.

Before broadcasting again, he gave the code signal to change transmission frequencies, then waited for his team to adjust their radios to ensure privacy. If their conversations were being monitored, this move would cut that off and let them communicate without being overheard by the Jones/Murray gang.

Daniel keyed his mic. "All DGTF, be advised we are now dealing with a hostage situation and a shot has been fired. Perpetrator and victims, plural, are in the black sedan stopped next to the trucks in front of the warehouse."

Putting it into words made his gut twist like he'd literally been punched in the stomach. Nevertheless, he stayed focused, gesturing at the officer beside him to emphasize the order.

"Jack Donadio is going to contact the other department heads and get a consensus. Hopefully they will agree. Our original plans to wait to make arrests have to change. We can't let these vehicles leave the scene. I want all exit roads blocked by whatever patrol cars are in position. Move. Now."

As Daniel finished speaking, he looked to Jack and saw his thumbs-up sign. So far, so good. "Stay on this frequency for the present," Daniel continued to broadcast. "If we need to change again, go to our second alternative channel."

Once he was certain the task force had been fully notified, he turned his attention to the scene. Apparently, someone had given an order to go dark after the single gunshot because the transport trucks had turned off their headlights and the lights in and around the warehouse blinked off leaving only the waxing moon to provide illumination. The siege was on.

"Units to the east and south, spotlights and flares please. DGTF, be advised I will be approaching the kidnap car on foot. Hold your fire."

"Copy" and "affirmative" answers came. Daniel paused to speak with Jack. "You hold your position unless I need you. Your discretion."

Jack gaped. "You're really going to just walk up to them?"

"What else do you suggest?"

"Maybe wait for a hostage negotiator?"

"How long will that take in the middle of the night? Someone could already be injured."

"At least call them back and try to find out what happened when we heard that shot."

He palmed his cell phone and pressed the preset for his grandmother's number. It rang three times before it was answered. No one spoke.

"This is Special Agent Daniel Slater, ATF," he began. "You're surrounded. Come out with your hands up."

The hysterical sounding female laugh over the phone gave him chills. "That's what you need to do, Agent."

"Is someone injured?"

"The gunshot? No, your granny just got uppity. But I have plenty more bullets where that one came from."

Despite it being a taunt, the reply pleased Daniel. Assuming the kidnapper was telling the truth, his loved ones were unhurt. Heaving a sigh, he raised a thumbs-up sign to Jack.

"Let me speak with her."

"No way. Tell you what, I'll put the other one on and you can talk to her."

Other one? A chill skittered up Daniel's spine and raised the short hair at the nape of his neck. What he had suspected and feared was apparently true. Whoever had taken Catherine and Joy had also taken Aurora. His entire life was in the balance.

A surprisingly strong, "Hello," confirmed his fears.

"Aurora. What happened? Is everybody really okay?"

"So far. There's an older gray-haired woman here. I don't recognize her but she says her name is Ingrid and she knows you."

In the background, he heard a string of shouted cursing followed by Aurora's gasp. "It's… She's… She says she's Brandon and Hal Murray's *mother*."

His blood turned to ice. "She can't be. Ingrid Murray is dead."

"Uh-uh. That's who she just said she was," Aurora told him. "Couldn't you hear her?"

Unfortunately, he had. "All right. What does she want?" The sound of a scuffle came to him rather than a spoken answer.

Ingrid had the phone again. "I want *you*, Agent Slater. I'm in charge now. You're going to pay for killing my Hal."

Daniel's heart sank. Hal Murray was a casualty of a prior shootout and also Brandon's older brother. It sounded plausible that this actually was Ingrid, even though she'd been reported as deceased for years. This turn of events explained a lot. Hotheaded Brandon had not been following his late brother's premade plans as they'd surmised. The brains behind the gun trafficking ring was Ingrid. Perhaps it had been under her leadership all along. That explained a lot. Brandon might not have the brains to keep running the operation successfully but his mother clearly did.

"We're always sorry when there is loss of life," Daniel said soberly. "The incident concerning Hal's death was fully investigated and the agents who were involved were cleared of any wrongdoing."

"In your eyes, maybe. Not in mine," Ingrid rasped.

Daniel held the phone away from his ear and could still hear her clearly. When she stopped screaming epithets at him, he calmly resumed their conversation despite the rocks in the pit of his stomach and the slight tremor in his hands. It was one thing to be afraid for his own life and quite another to consider the lives of loved ones.

That special group included Aurora Martin, he realized. His feelings were undeniable. Like it or not, he loved her as much as he loved Catherine and Joy. Knowing the three were together in that car was the most devastating scenario he'd ever faced.

"If I agree to come over there, will you promise to release the others?"

Jack grabbed his free arm and shook his head. "No way."

Adamant, Daniel pulled free. Nobody was going to stop him from doing everything he could to rescue his family. He didn't intend to die in the process. Taking risks was sometimes necessary even for the most seasoned veteran, the difference being he was positive he had to. There was no other option.

Solemn and determined, he handed Dakota's leash to Jack.

"Keep her safe, will you. I don't want to have to worry about getting her shot too."

"Okay, but if this plan falls apart and I see a need, I'm sending her in."

"Fair enough. I just want to get close enough to disarm Ingrid. I don't think she'll start shooting until she's made me suffer more."

"Such as?"

Daniel's mouth was so dry he could hardly swallow. He coughed. "I think she's going to try to kill the people I love and make me watch."

Holding her breath, Aurora waited for an opportunity to fight back. If she had been the only one in the car with Brandon's unhinged mother, she'd have felt better about taking chances. With Joy and Catherine as companions, that wasn't an easy option. Still, perhaps she could trick their captor somehow.

Spotting the lone figure of a man emerging from the near darkness, she caught her breath. There was no need to wait to see his face. The commanding way he walked told her it was Daniel Slater. In the many hours they'd spent together, she had learned to recognize every little detail about him and had come to hold each of them close to her heart.

Mindful of Ingrid, Aurora kept her prayers for him silent and simply thought, *Please, Jesus.* The rest didn't need to be voiced. God knew exactly how she felt about this extraordinary man and his present actions reaffirmed those conclusions.

Her hand closed on the door handle. Unless she'd been imagining a click because she'd expected to hear one, the car doors had all unlocked when Ingrid first stepped out. Surprise escape was worth a try, particularly if her actions drew the vindictive woman's attention away from Daniel. It would have been comforting to discuss the plan with him, yes, but since that was impossible, she could only hope and pray she wasn't about to make things worse.

Afraid to move too quickly, Aurora caught Catherine's attention with her eyes and realized the clever woman was anticipating what she was going to do because she'd pulled Joy into her lap and was transferring her to the side opposite Aurora. That was as far away as she could put her and hopefully the safest place in the back seat.

Ingrid was reacting to Daniel's approach too. Gun at the ready, she started to open the driver's door again.

That was the opportunity Aurora had been waiting for. The overhead light flashed on. She pulled the door handle, listening for the latch.

Ingrid yelled at Daniel.

Aurora pushed open her door. Saw Ingrid start to turn back toward her. Let herself fall to the ground where she would be hidden. A bullet whooshed past her and imbedded itself in the metal wall of the warehouse.

Success? In a warped sense of the word, it was, Aurora decided. Part of her goal had been to draw attention away from Daniel and the others. The second part, which she was now living, was to escape being killed. Accomplishing that promised to be a lot harder.

Scrambling on all fours, she cleared the rear of the sedan, then rose to run.

Ingrid's "Stop or I shoot the kid" sent a jolt through Aurora that brought her to an immediate halt. She put a hand to the corrugated metal wall next to her to keep her balance, then slowly raised both hands before starting to turn around.

Ingrid had circled the car containing Catherine and Joy and was currently standing a mere twenty feet away from Aurora with the gun pointing straight at her.

Breathless, Aurora nodded. "Okay, okay. You win."

"That's better. Now get back over here."

As Aurora prepared to move, she noticed a blur of action on the opposite side of the kidnap car and had to bow her head to keep from staring. From cheering.

Joy was being saved!

NINETEEN

Bright beams from myriad spotlights on the surrounding police cars cut the darkness into a crisscross pattern making it difficult to see clearly but Daniel could hear well enough, especially since Ingrid Murray's voice was raised and raspy.

Her shout of "get back here" could mean only one thing. Ingrid's attention was on someone outside the car and she had stepped away. Gritting his teeth, he broke into a run.

The car loomed. Dropping into a crouch, he tried the rear door and was able to open it.

Little Joy fell into his arms, clinging to his neck. Catherine gave the child a push. "Go, go!"

"You too."

"No. I'll stay to help Aurora."

Daniel wanted to yell at her, to grab her hand and pull her to safety with him. There was not enough time. Milliseconds lay between escape and death. He knew it and Catherine knew it. She was right. His present duty was to carry little Joy out of danger. And it was breaking his heart.

Turning, staying hunched over the child so his vest and his body would help protect her, Daniel started away.

People in the distance were shouting. Cheering. Then the shooting started. As he rounded his own SUV and came face to face with Jack, he yelled, "Cease fire! There are still two hostages."

Gunfire died down with only a few more pops after his order. Winded and heavy-hearted, he dropped to his knees, still embracing the toddler. She was sniffling against his shoulder but unhurt and he patted her back through her warm coat. "It's okay, honey. You're okay."

"Where's Nana?" she asked, her voice thready.

"I'll go get Nana and Aurora soon. I promise. Right now I want you to get in my car with Dakota and help her be good. Okay?"

Jack was scowling. "You're going to take your K-9 out of service? I don't like that idea much. We might need her."

"I know, but…" Daniel saw his colleague's point. Still, he wanted to be certain nobody else could get to Joy. The child tried to solve the dilemma for him by saying, "I'll be good, Daddy."

Daniel almost lost it right then and there. Pulling himself together he radioed for Jenna Morrow to join them.

"Why her? Why not Lucy? She has a young daughter," Jack asked.

"Jenna's the queen of snack food? Who better to keep a kid occupied?"

"We might need her Augie."

"Right. We'll bring them both over. A second pair of eyes on Joy won't hurt."

"Okay. Then what?"

Daniel huffed. "What did Ingrid do while I was running?"

"Mostly cussed," Jack said. "I could hear her all the way over here. Then the lights came on in the car and she shoved Aurora back inside."

"Catherine wouldn't come with me when I grabbed Joy," Daniel reported, shaking his head sadly.

"That was probably for the best. Ingrid moved pretty fast once she realized you had the kid. She shot at you at least once before our units returned fire. If Catherine had been with you, running behind, she could very well have been hit."

"Or not," Daniel said. "It's too late to change things now. How many units do we have in all?"

"Our team is here except for Kenyon. He's on his way, ETA ten. Local police sent in five cars with two more guarding possible escape routes. I'm not sure where your ATF people are."

"Okay. What about the negotiator?"

"No word yet. I turned that over to Chief Ross. He said he'd see what he could do but no guarantees."

"I copy."

Jenna's arrival in a Cold River patrol car was accompanied by Lucy Lopez in a Fargo unit. They parked on either side of Daniel's vehicle and got out. He greeted them with Joy in his arms. "I'm assigning you two to temporary babysitting duty."

Jenna rolled her eyes. "Because we're women?"

He almost laughed in spite of the situation. "No, because you always have enough candy and snacks with you to feed our whole team and she's Annalise's mother," he said, noting Lucy's proud expression.

Daniel heard Jenna chuckling as she and Lucy helped the toddler into the back seat of one of the cars. Then he turned to Jack. "Any reports of injuries after all that shooting?"

"Not on our side. I'm not sure about Ingrid. She was pretty exposed when it started."

"Let's find out." As Daniel lifted his cell phone, he pictured both Catherine and Aurora and prayed silently for their well-being.

The phone rang three times before someone answered. It was Catherine. "Danny?"

"Are you all right?"

"I am. Ingrid's arm is bleeding and Aurora is in the front seat giving her first aid."

Way to go, he thought. *Give us positions inside the car.*
"Copy. Anything else?"

"Yes, Ingrid isn't being rational."

"Hah! Says who?" echoed from the front seat.

"Says me," Catherine countered, lowering her voice a cupping the phone with her hand. "She doesn't seem to grasp is that this mess is her fault for involving her boys in this terrible business in the first place."

"It's always easier to blame somebody else," Daniel said, "especially the police. Can you tell how badly she's hurt?"

Catherine huffed. "Not bad enough to stop her if that's what you mean." She spoke even more quietly. "We're not dealing with a normal person here. She's totally unpredictable."

"Has she given you any idea of what she intends to do next?"

"You tell me. Listen." Screeching in the background was incoherent and unmistakably coming from Ingrid. Catherine sniffled and whispered, "Praise the Lord you got Joy out."

"I'll get the rest of you too," Daniel vowed. "Somehow."

"Well, if you don't, don't blame yourself. I know you'll do all you can. Don't go getting killed trying, okay? I'm too old to raise another child, especially by myself."

"I'll make it. We'll all make it," Daniel said. "How is Aurora doing? I saw her trying to escape. Too bad she got caught."

"Escape? Hah! That girl only ran to distract Ingrid. I don't think she ever expected to actually get away. And it worked. You were able to rescue our princess."

As Daniel's heart swelled with affection and pride, he also felt intense sorrow. Aurora was such a special woman. So smart. So loving. So willing to sacrifice. How could he have avoided falling in love with her?

The answer was plain. He couldn't have. And he hadn't. The time for declaring his independence was over. He needed a helpmate. A wife. And, God willing, he'd have the perfect woman as soon as this frightening test of wills was over.

Niggling doubt tried to sneak into his thoughts. He denied it. Aurora had been thrust into his life despite his prior decisions to remain single and proved by her mere presence that he'd been wrong. He did need someone. A particular someone.

He needed her. And he hadn't even told her so.

"I think it's stopped bleeding," Aurora told Ingrid. "Do you want me to help you put your arm back in the sleeve of your hoodie?"

"And grab my gun while you pretend to help? No thank you."

"I helped you take it off," she reminded the injured woman. "Please, don't you think this whole thing has gone too far? Isn't it time to give up and get some peace?"

"Peace? How will I have peace without my boy?"

"You still have Brandon. Don't you want to protect him?"

"Him? Your boyfriend killed the good one and left me with the dregs. Brandon never did have a brain in his head. It was Hal I was proud of. He was everything to me."

Thinking of the way Serena was treated by her absent father gave Aurora some empathy for Brandon Jones/Murray. No wonder he acted so desperate. He'd probably been trying to make up for not being like his brother his whole life.

Ingrid motioned Aurora away by waving the gun and transferred it to her injured side so she could reach over the seat toward Catherine. "Give me that phone."

Slowly, clearly reluctant, she handed the phone to their captor with the warning, "Daniel has us surrounded."

"Do you think I care? I was beyond that the instant I watched my Hal die."

"We all lose loved ones," Aurora said tenderly. "I recently lost my mother."

"Yeah, and your boyfriend's sister died. I heard. Too bad. I was going to help her along but there were police guards on her door."

"You got into the hospital?"

"Oh, yeah. Saw you too. You and the brat and that dumb-looking dog. Probably eats him out of house and home."

Racking her brain, Aurora couldn't picture seeing this woman when they'd visited Serena. Nevertheless, she could have been there. Everyone had been so concerned about losing Serena they probably weren't as conscious of their surroundings as they should have been.

"You let us go then. Let us go now."

"Very funny. You're a hoot." Ingrid pressed the phone to her ear. "Did you hear that, Mister ATF Agent? Me and my friends were all over that hospital and you walked right by us."

Was that true? Aurora wondered. Possibly. Although given Ingrid's obvious mental illness, it might also be an illusion. Where did wishful thinking stop and reality begin when a person was so distraught and confused?

Aurora didn't hear Daniel's reply but judging by the scowl on the older woman's face, he hadn't pleased her.

Ingrid pointed the cell phone at Aurora. "Ask your boyfriend to tell you what happened to my Hal?"

The option of speaking with Daniel again was too tempting to refuse. Aurora leaned toward the phone Ingrid still held. "Wh-what happened to him?"

Ingrid answered instead. "They buried him without me, that's what. I told Brandon to go claim Hal's body but he was too scared of the cops to listen to me so Hal was put in the ground all by himself." At this point, she began to weep. "My poor boy."

Aurora flashed a look at Catherine, hoping she'd understand, then made a grab for the gun, twisting it away and pulling on Ingrid's sore arm at the same time.

The cell phone fell onto the center console, bounced and slid onto the floor. Catherine lunged for Ingrid from the back seat and tried to grab her shoulders, missing, settling for a handful of hair instead, and pulling off a curly gray wig.

Surprisingly strong for someone her age, their captor continued to wrestle with Aurora until she was finally able to push her index finger through the trigger guard and fire another shot. The reaction of ejecting the spent shell propelled the top of the gun's receiver back almost as quickly as it discharged the bullet from the barrel. Aurora, hit by the action and injured, screamed and grabbed her stinging hand. Blood seeped from between her fingers. Unshed tears filled her eyes.

"Bit ya, did it?" Ingrid chortled. "Serves you right. I told you how this was going to go and I don't intend to change my mind so you might as well give up."

Catherine leaned over the front seat and waved the handful off fake hair. "You were wearing a wig?"

"Fooled ya, didn't I? Everybody was expecting an old lady so I gave them one. I had my boys in my teens. I'm far from over the hill."

Which explained why Ingrid was so strong, Aurora realized. They were facing a different enemy than she had expected. No wonder it had been so hard to disarm her.

Muttered conversation was coming from the cell phone on the floor. Ingrid motioned at Aurora with the gun barrel. "You. Pick it up and tell the cops I'm still in charge. If they try to rush us, I'll shoot you both, starting with you."

Aurora felt around with her good hand until her fingers brushed the phone. She raised it to her ear, hoping Daniel was still connected. "You heard?"

His voice sounded odd when he said, "Yes," as if he was fighting emotion, which made perfect sense to her since she was barely holding it together herself.

"I'm still in the front seat with Mrs. Murray. I bandaged her arm."

"Is she badly hurt? Are you?"

Aurora wanted to elaborate but thought better of it. "No. Not really. The action on her gun pinched my palm when she fired. Her arm is bandaged and not bleeding through."

"Copy. I heard everything she said. My team is holding in place to keep the guns from being moved while we wait for a hostage negotiator but they say it could be hours before one arrives. What do you think? Will she last that long?"

Before she snaps? Aurora added internally. She shook her head as if Daniel could see her. Their time was running out. This woman was not only injured, she was having some kind of mental episode making her doubly unstable. *Hours? No way.*

She cradled the phone with her uninjured hand while the other one throbbed and bled slightly. Then she answered his question the only way she could.

"No."

TWENTY

Out of viable options, Daniel told Aurora to hand the phone back to Ingrid. As soon as she did, he started to speak.

"Mrs. Jones, or is it Murray?"

"What's it to you?"

"Never mind. I have a proposition for you."

"I'm listening."

"It's me you're angry with, not my grandmother or the CSI tech, so why not make a trade?"

She huffed. "Yeah, right. What did you have in mind, Mister Special Agent?"

"Me. I'll show myself and start toward you. When you see me, you let the women go and we cross paths halfway. What do you say?" He had to work to keep from holding his breath. Offering exactly what he thought she wanted was his only choice, one he was willing to make for the well-being of his loved ones.

"I say…" She cursed colorfully, then laughed. "Wait. Let me put this on speaker again. I want everybody to hear you beg."

Daniel had hoped to avoid informing the hostages of his rescue plans until they were agreed on but there was nothing he could do to stop Ingrid.

"Okay. Talk. We're all listening," she said.

He cleared his throat and continued. "I don't see any alternative so I've offered to trade myself for the hostages."

As he had expected, both Aurora and Catherine raised a fuss. That seemed to delight their captor, much to Daniel's discouragement, so he directed his next remarks to them. "It's the only logical choice other than waiting this out and I can't see Ingrid changing her mind anytime soon."

She answered immediately. "You've got that right."

"Okay," he continued. "You agree to the trade?"

"I'm thinking about it," the gang leader drawled, increasing his anxiety. "Give me time to tell my men to back off. Then we'll see." Ingrid paused. "I'm gonna hang up now and get out of the car. If there's one single shot or if anybody tries to rush me, I'll put a bullet into granny. Got that?"

"Wait." Daniel radioed orders on the private channel, waiting for affirmative replies before assuring Ingrid she could safely leave her car and ending their conversation.

It was all he could do to keep from trembling visibly. He leaned back against his SUV for support and peered at the warehouse. A wind was rising, driving clouds across the waxing moon and lessening the visibility in waves. If the storm arrived in full force too soon, there was no telling how the dynamics of the standoff might change. That too was out of his control and he was feeling more and more helpless as the minutes passed.

He assessed the sky, then looked to Jack. "What's the latest weather report?"

"Not good. There's a cold front coming down from Canada."

"Snow?"

"Probably. Don't know how soon. Fargo already has two inches."

Daniel clenched his jaw and nodded. Snow was preferable to rain, although either could cause plenty of problems. Suppose he waited to see what developed before he took further action? Was that idea even viable?

As he and Jack watched, Ingrid slowly opened the driver's door of the sedan and got out. Except for the whistling wind, the night remained silent.

Instead of heading for the warehouse as Daniel had anticipated, Ingrid paused long enough to open the rear door and pull Catherine out, keeping hold of one of her arms while she pressed the gun into her ribs. There was no sign of Aurora.

His already pounding heart sped. His breathing was ragged. Puffs of condensation formed in front of his mouth and were immediately dispersed by the wind.

He reclaimed Dakota from his SUV, signaled wordless deployment orders to Jack and saw him nod and leave before turning back to stare at the scene developing in front of the warehouse. Without knowing where Aurora was and whether she was all right, he couldn't chance rushing Ingrid or letting any of his team do so no matter how much he wanted to end this siege once and for all.

Because he could no longer see Jack, Daniel figured nobody else could either. So far, so good. Still, Ingrid was keeping his grandmother close enough to kill her if she so chose.

At a loss and frustrated beyond words, Daniel suddenly realized what he had not done yet. He had not prayed. Not for wisdom. Not for assistance. Not for anything.

Starting with a plea for forgiveness, he raised his eyes to the heavens and began to call upon God. It didn't matter that he couldn't see a way out; he didn't have to. God willing, the way would be made clear.

Until then however, he was up to his chin in trouble and supposedly in charge. For the first time in memory, he was unsure of success and that frightened him more than anything else. Yes, he trusted the Lord to take care of His earthly children. And, yes, he knew Catherine and Aurora were believers.

But so was Serena. And regardless of countless fervent prayers for healing, God had chosen to take her home. That was part of the conundrum, wasn't it? Wanting to see one kind of result yet having to accept a contrary one wasn't as easy as it sounded when preachers tried to explain. Some things were beyond human understanding.

And, despite his desire to trust fully and leave problems in God's hands, he realized he wasn't having much success letting go of the ingrained desire to rush into danger for the sake of his loved ones. Sighing, he realized how true that thought was. He loved them both, and, sadly, only one of them knew it.

That changed the focus of his thoughts and prayers. "Lord, let me tell Aurora how I feel. Please? Somehow?

It must not be in front of Ingrid, he added. If that vindictive woman had any idea how deep his feelings ran, Aurora wouldn't stand a chance of surviving.

Left alone in the kidnapper's car, Aurora cradled her throbbing hand and tried to think. If she attempted to run away again, Ingrid would probably snap and shoot Catherine. If she just sat there, the two older women would likely return, which would prepare the way for Daniel to show himself. There wasn't any doubt that Ingrid intended to kill him. She'd already said so.

Aurora sighed with a shudder. At least her prayers for little Joy had been answered. The toddler was safe. The trouble was, if anything happened to Daniel Slater, the poor child would be parentless again. That was terrible to even imagine.

Moonlight was fading as storm clouds gathered, making it even harder for Aurora to see what she was doing in spite of the spotlights still shining from several police cars. Nevertheless, she was able to make out the dashboard. Something glinted to the right of the steering column. Her jaw dropped. Had Ingrid actually been careless enough to leave the key in the ignition? *No way.* And yet...

Opening the passenger door was out of the question. The

only way to reach the driver's seat was to climb over the center console on her left. In a perfect world, Aurora would have simply lifted herself over. Her bruised, bleeding hand might hamper her if she tried but so what? Enduring temporary pain would be worth it if she could gain an advantage.

Lifting her hips meant leaning on the seat and she felt the stickiness of blood beneath her palm. Pain shot up her arm, almost making her cry out. She bit her lower lip, tried again and succeeded.

Between the excitement and the agony, catching her breath was impossible. She slipped behind the wheel and dragged her right leg into position on the floor pedals. An idea was forming. It was off the wall, yes, but nothing about Ingrid's choices made sense and she was the one in charge. Maybe it was time to fight fire with fire, so to speak.

Aurora blinked and peered through the windshield. She could see Catherine and their captor standing beside one of the trucks. A small group of men had gathered there too, and she hoped one of them was Brandon Murray because his location was the only unknown at the moment. Figuring out where all her enemies were was impossible. One thing she did know. She was not about to sit there like a fake duck in a carnival shooting gallery and let some demented criminal end her life. Or those of people she cared about.

Thanking God that her right hand was uninjured, Aurora reached for the key. Once she started the car, there would be only seconds in which to act before Ingrid started shooting. Could she actually bring herself to drive into a crowd of people without knowing who she might hit? The answer was *no*.

Clumps of wet snow were beginning to fall, partially obliterating her already tenuous view of Catherine and her captors. That made deciding even harder.

A sharp rap on the opposite window startled Aurora so much that she almost keyed the starter. A face in shadow

waved to her. Knowing that one of Ingrid's men would definitely not be that subtle, she chanced lowering the electric
window.

Jack Donadio pressed a finger across his lips and leaned
closer to speak just above a whisper, "Come with me. I'll get
you out."

"I can't leave Catherine."

"Where is she?"

Aurora pointed through the snow flurries. "Over there. See
her? In the red scarf."

He nodded. "Suppose I can get Catherine off to one side.
Do you think you can crash this car into the front of the truck
as a diversion?"

"Yes."

"Okay. Do that when I signal, then immediately shift into
Reverse and back away as fast as you can. I'll take care of
Catherine."

Aurora's already pounding heart affirmed everything.
"What about Daniel? Is he okay? He said he was going to
walk right out in the middle of the parking lot."

"I'll notify him what's up by radio," Jack said. "We'd better hurry before somebody spots me."

"Right." With auxiliary power already engaged, Aurora
was able to close the window and use the front wipers to clear
the windshield without making any unnecessary noise. She
saw Jack, and Beau, working their way along the front of the
building in the deep shadows. The only easily visible color
was the white lettering on his and the dog's protective vests.
Trouble was, if she could see it, so could the gang members.

Hands fisted around the wheel so tightly her fingers began
to cramp, Aurora watched. Waited. Felt an urge to start the
car that almost overcame her.

Pain from her hand throbbed in time with her rapid heartbeats, marking time and counting down to action. She pressed

her lips into a thin line and gritted her teeth. An internal warning to fasten her seat belt came and was ignored. No way was she going to take her eyes off Catherine. Not for anything. She must know where Daniel's sweet grandmother was every second.

The red-scarfed figure began to slowly move to Aurora's right, feet shuffling sideways rather than taking actual steps.

Aurora reached for the ignition key. Her foot pressed the brake. Exterior stoplights flashed on the outside of the car. Ingrid flinched and started to turn.

That did it. Out of time and knowing she had no other way to launch an offensive that had a chance of working, Aurora turned the key. Two mechanical coughs. Accelerator to the floor. The engine roared. Tires squealed. The car leaped forward, wheels spinning and slewing in the wet snow.

Aurora's courage held. She wasn't vindictive like their kidnapper. She didn't want to hurt anyone. Not really. But something or someone had caused Ingrid to leave the key behind and Aurora wasn't about to question such good fortune. Call it divine guidance or simply a mistake on Ingrid's part, the result was the same. They were in a battle for their lives and the tide had turned.

The crash against the front bumper of the truck was metal against metal, snapping Aurora's head back and suggesting to her that she had not pinned anyone. At least she hoped not. Groggy, she blinked rapidly in an attempt to clear her head.

Bullets shattered the car's windshield. With nowhere else to go, she threw herself down across the front console. Jack had told her to back up after the crash but she hadn't had time.

Glass shattered. Bullets imbedded themselves in the car's upholstery. With every bang, Aurora expected to feel the hard hit of one of the projectiles.

Mindless of the pain in her injured hand, she pressed her

palms over her ears, muted the ambient sounds and turned her mind and body over to God. The time for fighting, for her at least, was past. Now, all she could do was wait to see who won.

TWENTY-ONE

Daniel was already running toward the warehouse with Dakota beside him when the shooting started. He'd received a brief report from Jack and had tried to deny Aurora permission to drive into the fray but by that time it had been too late.

His speed had increased the moment he saw the car start to move. Knowing that the woman he loved was behind the wheel gave him all the stamina he needed, and more. Mindless of the bullets flying, he dropped into a crouch to cover the final thirty feet, hit the driver's door with a bang, both hands splayed on the metal, and jerked it open.

In the background, he heard shouts of "Police. Hands up" and "Cease fire." Shooting stopped.

Someone was screaming. Others cursed. A few tried to run and were quickly tackled. Daniel ignored them all. As his hand gripped the door handle, his heart was hopeful. If he'd been a gambling man, he'd have refused to bet that whoever was still in that bullet-riddled car was unhurt. Nevertheless, he couldn't bring himself to imagine otherwise.

He opened the door farther and crouched behind it with the panting Dane at his side. Aurora lay draped across the seats. When he grabbed her ankle, intending to pull her out, she screamed.

Daniel had never heard a more welcome sound in his whole life.

"Aurora!"

"Daniel!"

Giving a tug, he slid her closer, then opened his arms as she swiveled and reached for him. Breathless, speechless, he pulled her into a tight embrace, noting that she was holding onto him just as desperately.

Stroking her hair and gasping for air, he began kissing the top of her head as it lay against his chest. Finally, he managed, "Are you hurt?"

"J-just my hand," he stuttered. "Catherine? Is she okay?"

"She must be. I saw Jack move her out of the way before you…" He bit back a sob. "Oh, honey, why did you put yourself in such danger? I told you I'd get you out."

"You never said I couldn't help."

How could he be upset with her when he was so overjoyed to know she'd survived? Brief introspection proved that his anger was more about himself—and the friend and team member who had had last contact with her.

"Jack put you up to it, didn't he?"

Aurora relaxed her hold enough to look up at him. "I was already behind the wheel when I saw him, so not exactly. My plan was to do something with the car as soon as your grandmother was clear. Jack arranged that."

Rolling his eyes, Daniel felt a tear rolling down his chilled cheek and swiped it away. Snow was continuing to fall, catching in Aurora's hair and glistening with points of light like stars in a night sky.

Starting to speak, he faltered, coughed, then found his voice. "I thought I'd lost you."

Her hug had been loosening. It tightened again when he said, "I love you, Aurora."

Because she didn't echo the tender sentiment, Daniel feared she wasn't going to. In the trauma of the moment, had he overstepped? Was she going to reject his declaration? Could he take it if she did?

Those questions were answered when she pushed away, rose to her knees, cupped his face and kissed him. Returning that kiss was easy. Ending it was not. As soon as she started to pull away, he held her more tightly, more possessively, in spite of his desire to take his time and make sure they were both as committed as he was.

A head popped around the side of the car door. It was Jack. "I was going to ask if you two were okay but it looks like you're fine."

Although he kept an arm around Aurora's shoulders, Daniel replied. "Pretty good, actually." He had to smile. "Status report?"

"Scene is secure. Catherine is shaken but uninjured. We have Ingrid and her henchmen in custody. The trucks are filled to the top with illegal firearms and ammo. One of the drivers has already offered to provide names and numbers for the people on the receiving end of their delivery and he says there are half a dozen lockers still crammed full in a storage block behind the office inside. It's a massive haul."

"Great." Helping Aurora, Daniel got to his feet and dusted off snow. Much to his relief, she stayed glued to his side, her arm around his waist, while Dakota took her place beside him too. "What about Brandon?"

"We haven't ID'd all the gang members in custody." Jack frowned. "Come to think of it, I don't recall seeing him."

"Then we have a loose end," Daniel said, reaching for his radio. "All units, be advised. Brandon Jones/Murray may be at large. Use caution. He's known to be armed and dangerous."

When Aurora glanced up at him, Daniel felt bathed in so much affection it staggered him. What he wanted to do was take her somewhere private where they could discuss their future. It had to be spent together. It just had to be. Anything else was unthinkable.

"I need to take you back to Joy," he told her. "Jenna and Lucy are watching her for me. Over there where I'm parked."

"What about Catherine?" Aurora asked.

How like the special woman he knew she was, Daniel thought. Always thinking of others. He looked to Jack. "Bring Nana over too, will you? I want to keep my family all in one place."

"Copy that."

"I'll wait for her," Aurora said. "She was so brave."

"So were you. I'm really proud of you," he said, beginning to smile slightly. "Just promise me you won't do anything like that again."

"I hope I never have to." There were unshed tears in her eyes. "It was terrible thinking I might actually hurt somebody, even if they were threatening to harm us." A blush rose to paint her cheeks even more than the icy wind already had. "Say it again?"

"Say what again? No more wild driving?"

"No. The part about family. I keep thinking I heard you say something about love too."

"I did. And you are family. At least I hope you will be someday soon."

"Like, officially?"

Nodding, he placed a kiss on her forehead. "Yes. Officially. Give that some serious thought while we gather up my grandmother, will you?"

"Hey! That's right," Aurora said, grinning. "I'll have a new gramma too. Bonus relatives."

Daniel sobered. "About that. Family, I mean. Are you ready to become Joy's mother?"

"If you're her father."

"Very soon." Daniel kept expecting Jack to appear with Catherine in tow so he was reluctant to say much more. Yes, he planned to officially propose to Aurora but not here. Not like this. A proposal needed to be romantic to please a woman, at least he assumed it did. Not that he'd had oodles of practice. Besides, this whole concept of having a wife was new to him. He hadn't had time to buy a ring, let alone think up a flowery speech.

Daniel's radio interrupted his thoughts, making them jump, Dakota included. He tightened up on the leash and answered. "Slater."

It was Jack. "I can't find Catherine. She was right here a minute ago but she's not now. Nobody seems to know where she went. Is she with you?"

"No," Daniel said. "You were the last one to see her. Are you sure she's missing?"

"I'm standing here in an empty space, boss."

"Okay. I'll be right there."

"We'll be right there," Aurora added.

"No way, lady. You're going to stay with Jenna, Lucy and Joy while I search with Dakota and my team." He watched her jaw drop as she stared at him so he softened his commands. "I need to know you're secure in order to keep my focus, Aurora. Do it for Nana's sake, not because I said you had to. Please?"

She sighed and shrugged. "That's better. Okay. Over there?" she asked, pointing at his SUV.

"Yes. I'll drop you off with Joy. As soon as we get eyes on my grandmother, I'll radio and we'll know this whole operation is wrapped up." The slump of her shoulders told him she was going to comply without further argument. Seeing that was an immense relief, almost as great as knowing they had nearly ended the Dakota gun trafficking ring. One more piece of the puzzle and it would truly be over.

He took her elbow and started guiding her across the parking area in front of the warehouse. Falling snow partially blocked his view of his and Jenna's vehicles but he knew where they were. Wet snow squeaked beneath their boots with every fresh step. The wind had picked up, driving the falling clumps almost horizontally.

Aurora pulled up the hood on her parka and shivered. "Whoa. That's cold."

"And predicted to get worse," Daniel said. "You'll be warm enough once you're in the car with Joy and the others."

"I hate to imagine poor Catherine out in this," Aurora said. "Find her? Quickly?"

"We will." He waved to Jenna to unlock the car doors and was relieved to see Joy welcome Aurora as if she had been waiting and hoping for her to come. He leaned in before closing the door. "Keep everybody here with you two until I can bring Catherine. Understand?"

"Copy," Lucy said, peering past him at the falling snow. "Where is she?"

Daniel shook his head just enough to warn his team members to stop asking questions he didn't want to answer in front of his soon-to-be daughter. "Later."

"Gotcha." Jenna made eye contact with Lucy and Aurora, then swung her gaze back to Daniel. "Go. We'll be fine."

If he had not believed that with all his heart, he knew he wouldn't have been able to back away. Straightening, he hitched up Dakota's leash to keep her close, turned and started back toward the warehouse.

Dakota seemed reluctant which Daniel attributed to the icy wind and snow. He'd make sure she was well warmed up soon. First, they had a job to do. He gave a slight tug and the command to heel.

Although Dakota obeyed, she continued to do so haltingly, looking from side to side and sniffing the air.

A chill snaked up Daniel's spine and prickled the hair at the nape of his neck. Yes, he was feeling the cold but this was different somehow. Eerie. As his mind whirled, he realized that he'd been so intent on returning to his team at the warehouse he'd failed to heed what his K-9 was trying to tell him.

Torn between standard operating procedures and instinct, he paused and listened. Wind and snow were muting ambient sounds so much he couldn't hear well. Dakota however apparently heard or smelled or sensed something that was escaping him.

Pivoting, he looked back at the Cold River patrol car where he'd left two of his loved ones. Not much was visible except for the presence of human forms beside the car.

Someone keyed a mic. Broadcasting voices sounded distant until he heard Jenna's "Mayday," followed by Aurora clearly saying, "Put the gun down. Don't hurt Catherine. I'll come with you."

The urge to shout, "No!" was almost too strong to deny. Daniel mentally calculated the distance to the car, reached to unclip Dakota and gave her the command to attack, trusting her to see the gun and target the hand holding it.

The Dane took off like a greyhound in the race of her life with Daniel right behind. She disappeared for a second, hidden by the falling snow. He heard a shot. His heart nearly burst. He couldn't feel his feet or leg muscles. His lungs ached as gulps of icy air made them sting and protest.

Pushing through the pain, he drew closer and saw Jenna's car clearly. Interior lights shined out the open doors and multiple figures were wrestling in the falling snow. At least one was screaming. Others were shouting.

Jenna and Lucy on either side of the central figures were flung away like limp rags. Muzzle flash sliced through the night air showing a bullet traveling skyward. Dakota instantly leaped for the arm holding the gun and deflected a second shot.

Right behind him, Daniel shouted, "Hands up! You're under arrest. It's over."

Fighting on, Brandon Murray kept hold of Catherine's wrist

and braced against the patrol car while Dakota struggled to pull him down.

Daniel reached for the revolver in the attacker's hand and tore it away just as one of the car doors was flung open and knocked Brandon to his knees.

Recovering themselves, Jenna and Lucy dived on top of him while Dakota continued to bite his arm and he screeched like a demented hawk.

"Out!" Daniel commanded Dakota, aiming his own firearm at Brandon to give the female officers a chance to handcuff him.

Aurora was out of the car and grinning as she embraced Catherine. Watching the two women he loved most in the world expressing affection brought unshed tears to his already freezing lashes.

He keyed his radio. "We've got Brandon Murray in custody and hostages are safe. You can all stand down."

Beaming proudly, the older woman sidled up to embrace him as soon as he'd holstered his gun. Aurora was right behind her. "Is that it?" she asked. "Or are there more crooks you'd like us to help you catch?"

Scowling down at them, he wanted to deliver a lecture, to berate her and Catherine for risking their lives. He didn't do it. Couldn't do it. Not when he was so overjoyed to see them both alive and well.

And speaking of Joy. Daniel's heart swelled with love and thanksgiving as he led everyone closer to the police car and scooped up the toddler.

"Good Doo-dah," she chortled, clapping her hands the way she'd seen her great grandmother celebrate.

"Yes, good Dakota," Aurora said, smiling through tears. "She came out of nowhere and saved us."

Daniel was abashed to recall how he had almost ignored his K-9 partner's signals. He wouldn't make that mistake again.

* * *

As other officers led the handcuffed man away and Jenna drove off with Lucy, Daniel carefully dried Dakota's wet, icy paws in the rear of his SUV before removing her working vest and offering her favorite toy as a reward for a job well done.

There was no safe way to haul everyone he wanted to keep with him so he radioed Jack to see if he was almost finished at the warehouse.

"Affirmative. CSIs will be taking this place apart for the rest of the night. I can shake loose. Why?"

"I need to trade cars so I have seating for all my passengers. You can follow us back to the station with Dakota and Beau."

"Good thing they're pals," Jack said. "Come to think of it, it's a good thing you and I are too. I don't let just anybody drive my special-issue wheels."

"Thanks, man. I appreciate it."

"You're welcome. Actually, you kind of surprise me. I'd have thought you'd want to be alone with a certain lady."

Heaving a noisy sigh, Daniel looked over at Aurora. She and Catherine were both cuddling Joy, sharing love and warmth. The sight of them together was an image he'd never forget.

Daniel lowered his voice for privacy. "I want to do it right. Woman expect the perfect proposal."

Jack laughed so raucously Daniel figured he must have caught everyone's attention. "You're joking, right?"

"No. Not at all."

"Okay. Have it your way. But if it was me, I'd stop finding excuses and ask her now, when she's still thinking of you as her hero."

Eye contact with Aurora showed Daniel that she'd overheard enough to get the gist of their conversation. He keyed the mic. "Just get over here with those keys before we freeze to death."

Catherine took possession of Joy and said, "We'll warm up in your car with Dakota while you take care of business."

That left little room for stalling. Nevertheless, Daniel wasn't sure his friend was right. He wanted his marriage to last for a lifetime and assumed getting the proper start would make a difference.

Facing Aurora, he spread his hands, palms up, and shrugged. "Well, I don't know what to say next."

"Neither do I," she said quietly, approaching him until they stood mere inches apart. "None of my plans seem to fit what's going on here."

"Us, you mean?"

"Uh-huh. Confusing, isn't it?"

"Very," he said softly.

A blush heightened the already rosy color of her cheeks beneath the sides of her hood while tendrils of golden hair blew across her face. Daniel whisked them away with one finger before leaning in for a kiss.

"Um, nice. That helps," Aurora said moments later. "But we need to be sensible. We'll have a lot of changes to make. Can you do that?"

"Can *you*?" he asked, holding his breath until she answered.

"It will be a pleasure." She started to smile. "Probably not easy all the time but definitely doable."

"I think so too," Daniel said, cupping her cheeks and tilting her face up for another kiss. "Aurora Martin, will you marry me?"

As soon as she started to nod, he pulled her into a tight embrace and kissed her again.

When they came up for air, he heard her whisper, "Yes," against his cheek and he began to understand what it meant to be part of a true family.

EPILOGUE

Aromas of roasting turkey, sage dressing and apple pie filled the kitchen and wafted into the dining room of the Slater home. Aurora would have been nervous hosting Daniel's DGTF team for Thanksgiving if Catherine hadn't taken charge of preparing most of the food.

Jack arrived early with Beau and unofficially appointed himself to doggy duty by welcoming arriving K-9s to the enclosed garage and supervising play for the dogs who were known to get along socially.

West Cole and Trish brought their son, Gabriel, who was about eight months younger than Joy. Aurora helped Trish set up a play area for the younger children, including the three-year-old Graves twins, Beacon and Austin, who arrived with Kenyon Graves and his new bride, Raina McCord. Lucy Lopez's little girl, Annalise, who was four going on fourteen, appointed herself activities director and was trying to convince the younger children to play games her way. It was a happy bedlam and Raina McCord, who was now the twins' official mother, kept an eye on her boys.

Following Catherine's suggestion after seeing the guest list, Aurora had set up the dining table as a buffet. The children would eat at the kitchen table with a few of the adults while others could choose seating on chairs or sofas in the open living areas. It was the best she could do with so many to feed.

Daniel came up behind her as she was fussing over an arrangement of cutlery on the linen tablecloth. "If they run out of forks, they can use their fingers," he quipped. "The kids will, anyway."

"You've been hanging around dogs too long," she countered. "Some of us are actually civilized."

He laughed, warming her heart. The mere sight of him made her heart speed. Hearing and seeing him so happy, so content, Aurora was thrilled to her core. "Are they all here?"

"Not quite," he said. "Isabella and Liam texted they're on their way. Zach and Eden will be a little late too. He says Eden's moving slower and slower with their baby due so soon."

"What about Jenna? I haven't seen her since the night at the warehouse."

"She had to go back to work in Cold River now that the gun traffickers have been taken down, so she and Clay Miller are celebrating on his ranch."

"I'm glad they're happy." She met Daniel's gaze. "I'd feel guilty if we were the only ones." As she'd intended, that made him laugh again.

"The ones who aren't happy are Ingrid and Brandon," Daniel said, sobering as he spoke. "It's hard to believe we brought down the whole organization but it looks like we did just that. Justice is served and the charges are sure to put them away for a long time."

"I know. I'm so proud of you." She looked around at the crowd. "All of you."

"And our K-9s," Daniel added. "They're very special."

"Yes, they are. I still get the shivers when I picture Dakota leaping on Brandon. She practically disarmed him single-handedly."

"If she had thumbs and could work handcuffs, she could have made the arrest," Daniel said. "You weren't so bad yourself. When you shoved that car door into him and he hit the ground, it was all over."

"You'd have managed without me. I just had a strong urge to do something. I don't plan to make a practice of interfering." Aurora stepped into his embrace and laid her head on his chest, listening to the beat of his heart and reveling in the knowledge she was loved so totally.

"Good to hear." Daniel checked his watch, then raised his arm and made an announcement. "Listen up, people. Gather around the laptop on the coffee table. Our very own technical guru Cheyenne Chen has worked one of her computer tricks to keep their location secret and I have a special surprise for you."

Daniel had told Aurora what was coming and because she had never met Cameron Holmes, or whatever his current WIT-SEC name was, she backed off to leave room for the others behind and next to him. Two grinning faces appeared on his screen. Someone gasped. "Gracie!"

"That's right," Daniel said. "Lorelei, Gracie's the US marshal who was with our team before your assignment here. She and Cameron are in witness protection together now."

Lorelei Danvers leaned over Daniel's shoulder to wave. "Hi, Gracie. I'm sorry you had to leave the DGTF but I'm glad I got to be part of this super group."

"Cam and I are happy here so it all worked out." She giggled. "Never mind where *here* happens to be. Marriage agrees with us."

"Obviously."

Gracie was grinning and so was her rancher husband. "I was surprised to hear from you guys," she said. "They tell me the Jones gang's been stopped for good. Are you all going your separate ways or is the team staying together?"

Daniel answered. "It depends. We'll all go back to our regular jobs for now. If another special assignment comes up, I know where to find the best of the best."

"That you do." She raised her hands into view of the camera and applauded. "Great job."

"On behalf of all of us, thanks," Daniel said. "Remember Joy, the toddler we found the month before you left? I'm adopting her."

"Terrific."

"And getting married," Catherine called out from the kitchen.

Daniel chuckled. "Yup. And getting married. There's a lot of that kind of thing going around. Lucy and Micah Landon are engaged, Zach and Eden Kelcey are back together, and the FBI agent, Liam Barringer. Remember him? He eloped with forensic artist Isabella Whitmore."

At Gracie's "Good grief," the group gathered for the video call laughed.

"I know, I know. Unbelievable, isn't it?"

He paused, apparently thinking, while Aurora grinned from ear to ear, delighted to be a part of the romantic plague taking over Plains City and beyond.

"Oh, and remember Kenyon Graves? He's not dead. He had amnesia and has recovered enough to join us for the wrap-up of this case."

"What about his boys? Twins, weren't they?"

Kenyon leaned forward to explain, "Growing like weeds. My friend Raina is their legal mother now that we're married."

"I'm delighted for all of you," Gracie said. "Cam and I both are thrilled, even if that isn't his name anymore." She laughed again. "You have no idea how hard it is to take on a totally new persona and remember all the details when people ask about your personal history."

"I'm sure leaving the past behind is hard," Daniel said. He glanced over his shoulder at Aurora. "But sometimes that's the only way to go forward."

"Amen to that," Jack shouted from across the room.

Bathed in laughter and surrounded by the people who had been virtual strangers mere months ago, Aurora grinned. As part of her healing, she had phoned her father and invited him to join their current celebration. Although he had made other plans for that particular day, he had promised to visit soon—and to bring the woman he was currently dating. To Aurora's surprise she was looking forward to their reunion and hadn't felt more than a tiny twinge of concern about his inclusive suggestion. The only other thing she wished was that Daniel's father was here so they too could make their peace.

Daniel ended the video call, closed the laptop and stood. "Okay. Who would like to say the blessing on the meal? I'm starving and I imagine you all are too."

West Cole spoke up. "I'll do it. And while I'm at it, I want to give thanks for something else too." He grinned at Trish who was balancing little Gabriel on one hip. "We're going to have a playmate for our son in the spring."

Amid congratulations, Aurora found her way to Daniel's side and slipped an arm around his waist. Despite danger and loss and unavoidable change, they had found each other. Without the influence from the problems that had seemed so overwhelming, perhaps they would have gone on with their solitary, lonely lives, never dreaming that such happiness and well-being waited just out of reach.

As West bowed his head and blessed the food, Aurora added a silent prayer of her own, thanking God for her life, her future husband and the darling little girl she would soon call her own. She also thanked Him for the selfless sacrifices of Serena who had practically set it up, in more ways than one, when she'd brought joy into their lives. The name she had chosen fit perfectly. Joy. A gift beyond words.

* * * * *

*If you enjoyed Daniel's story, don't miss Cheyenne's
and Lorelai's stories next! Check out* Christmas K-9 Patrol
and the rest of the Dakota K-9 Unit series!

Chasing a Kidnapper
by Laura Scott, April 2025

Deadly Badlands Pursuit
by Sharee Stover, May 2025

Standing Watch
by Terri Reed, June 2025

Cold Case Peril
by Maggie K. Black, July 2025

Tracing Killer Evidence
by Jodie Bailey, August 2025

Threat of Revenge
by Jessica R. Patch, September 2025

Double Protection Duty
by Sharon Dunn, October 2025

Final Showdown
by Valerie Hansen, November 2025

Christmas K-9 Patrol
by Lynette Eason and Lenora Worth, December 2025

*Available only from Love Inspired Suspense
Discover more at LoveInspired.com*

Dear Reader,

When I was asked to write Book 8 in this series and deal with events surrounding hospice care, I didn't know that a dear friend was going to leave this earth the same way before I had finished the manuscript. I actually lost two very good friends at almost the same time. It shook me. Then I remembered my personal conviction that God is in the details and nothing happens without His influence; not my writing successes, my family, my growing circle of friends, nothing. Not even loss.

The expressions of faith and simple approaches Aurora used to explain life and death from a Christian perspective are not new concepts to me. I used them with my very young nephews when their grandpa, my father, died, and have extensive experience with kindergartners. Because I was a classroom aide and not a teacher, I was able to take extra time to comfort grieving little ones. To cry with them. To let them be themselves and work through their pain, one step at a time.

That's what we all must do. There is no right or wrong way to grieve and no time limit for healing. Each person we love takes a part of us with them when they go. The future changes. We change. It's inevitable. But once we step across that black abyss of sorrow and put a foot on the path to the rest of our lives, we give ourselves a chance to find out what else is in store for us.

The rest of our days don't have to be mournful. We'll never forget or stop loving the ones who have gone ahead of course, but I think we owe it to them to live the best life possible. Until we all meet again.

Blessings,
Valerie Hansen
Val@ValerieHansen.com

Get up to 4 Free Books!

**We'll send you 2 free books from each series you try
PLUS a free Mystery Gift.**

Both the **Love Inspired®** and **Love Inspired® Suspense** series feature compelling
novels filled with inspirational romance, faith, forgiveness and hope.

YES! Please send me 2 FREE novels from the Love Inspired or Love Inspired Suspense series and my FREE gift (gift is worth about $10 retail). After receiving them, if I don't wish to receive any more books, I can return the shipping statement marked "cancel." If I don't cancel, I will receive 6 brand-new Love Inspired Larger-Print books or Love Inspired Suspense Larger-Print books every month and be billed just $7.19 each in the U.S. or $7.99 each in Canada. That is a savings of 20% off the cover price. It's quite a bargain! Shipping and handling is just 50¢ per book in the U.S. and $1.25 per book in Canada.* I understand that accepting the 2 free books and gift places me under no obligation to buy anything. I can always return a shipment and cancel at any time by calling the number below. The free books and gift are mine to keep no matter what I decide.

Choose one:
☐ **Love Inspired
Larger-Print**
(122/322 BPA G36Y)

☐ **Love Inspired
Suspense
Larger-Print**
(107/307 BPA G36Y)

☐ **Or Try Both!**
(122/322 & 107/307 BPA G36Z)

Name (please print)

Address _____ Apt. #

City _____ State/Province _____ Zip/Postal Code

Email: Please check this box ☐ if you would like to receive newsletters and promotional emails from Harlequin Enterprises ULC and its affiliates. You can unsubscribe anytime.

Mail to the **Harlequin Reader Service:**
IN U.S.A.: P.O. Box 1341, Buffalo, NY 14240-8531
IN CANADA: P.O. Box 603, Fort Erie, Ontario L2A 5X3

Want to explore our other series or interested in ebooks? Visit www.ReaderService.com or call 1-800-873-8635.

*Terms and prices subject to change without notice. Prices do not include sales taxes, which will be charged (if applicable) based on your state or country of residence. Canadian residents will be charged applicable taxes. Offer not valid in Quebec. This offer is limited to one order per household. Books received may not be as shown. Not valid for current subscribers to the Love Inspired or Love Inspired Suspense series. All orders subject to approval. Credit or debit balances in a customer's account(s) may be offset by any other outstanding balance owed by or to the customer. Please allow 4 to 6 weeks for delivery. Offer available while quantities last.

Your Privacy—Your information is being collected by Harlequin Enterprises ULC, operating as Harlequin Reader Service. For a complete summary of the information we collect, how we use this information and to whom it is disclosed, please visit our privacy notice located at https://corporate.harlequin.com/privacy-notice. Notice to California Residents – Under California law, you have specific rights to control and access your data. For more information on these rights and how to exercise them, visit https://corporate.harlequin.com/california-privacy. For additional information for residents of other U.S. states that provide their residents with certain rights with respect to personal data, visit https://corporate.harlequin.com/other-state-residents-privacy-rights/.

LIRLIS25